# SHEPPARD

## Marshall's Shadow Book 1

# KATHI S. BARTON

This is a work of fiction. Names, characters, places, and incidents are products of the author's imagination or are used fictitiously and are not to be construed as real. Any resemblance to actual events, locations, organizations, or persons, living or dead, is entirely coincidental.

**World Castle Publishing, LLC**
Pensacola, Florida
Copyright © Kathi S. Barton 2019
Paperback ISBN: 9781950890149
eBook ISBN: 9781950890156
First Edition World Castle Publishing, LLC, June 3, 2019
http://www.worldcastlepublishing.com
**Licensing Notes**
Cover: Karen Fuller
Editor: Maxine Bringenberg

# Chapter 1

Sheppard Marshall, with hat in hand, made his way to the front of the church. His ma, dead these three days, was awaiting her place in her Garden of Eden that she had talked about all the time. He hadn't been home as much as he should have, all because of work.

Shep figured he'd held up the pall bearers enough, so decided to get on with it.

Kneeling down, he put large rough hands on the smooth oak casket. The beautiful spray of roses was lain over her like one of the quilts that she made every year. He knew that in the last few of them, she'd barely been able to walk to the table, much less sit at her quilter. Wiping at the tears that he'd shed more in the last three days than he had in his life, he started to speak to her as if she were sitting in her little rocker snapping beans for supper.

"Ma, I'm surely sorry I didn't make it like I thought I could. I talked to the other boys. They said you were in a car accident. I'm so sorry that I couldn't be here for you." There was plenty for Sheppard to be sorry for, he thought. A longer list than he thought that his ma knew about. He smiled then. For sure, she knew each and every one of his deeds. "I'm sure you and the good Lord know each thing I did, even if I thought to keep them from you."

His ma was gone. His heart broke every time he thought about her not being there when he called home. He'd tried his best to make sure she had a good ending. Sending her money every payday had helped her, he knew that. Also having her put in one of them homes that she'd get round the clock care had kept her safe. But Shep knew he'd not been able to give her the one thing she wanted — a wife for him and a grandchild for her.

When he was ready to face the cemetery, he got up and walked to the back of the big church. In his lifetime he thought he'd polished more of those pews than most people his age. All his fidgeting that had been done in the seats had made them shiny well beyond what polish could have done.

Dean and his other brothers were there waiting for him when he stepped into the sunlight.

"I thought for sure you weren't going to make it." Sheppard told his brother Oakley that he'd had to pull in a few favors to make it home. "Are you home for good this time, Shep? Dad is around. Grandda told me the other day that he was."

"Causing any trouble?" He didn't answer the question about staying home this time. Shep thought he'd made it clear that he was — his boss was a shit hole and Sheppard wasn't sure he was keen on working. Shep had been doing his work and his boss's for the last several years. Rodney told him that their dad hadn't caused trouble so far. "I don't know what

I'm doing, to be honest with you."

The funeral director asked them to get into the limo. Shep eyed the machine and wondered if the man had gotten a good look at them. They were big men. The thought of crushing into that thing gave him the willies.

"Mr. Marshall, we have two limos for the family." Nodding at the man, Trenton, Heath, and Rodney got into one limo. Shep, Dean, and Oakley got into the second one. "There is no one else, correct?"

Dean said that it was just the six of them and the door was shut. Asking his brothers about their father, he settled back in the seat, trying his best to straighten his tie. Oakley turned toward him and fixed it for him as he spoke.

"Dad has been around the farm a couple of times. Usually when no one is there. But since you had us put that surveillance shit around, we just have to call the cops when the thing goes off. Sure did scare the shit out of me the first time I heard it." Shep leaned back in the seat when Oakley had the tie looking better. "Since they have an idea who he is and what sort of crap he might be doing, they're out there before he can do any damage. The last time Dad fell and had to wait for someone to help him up. Drunk as hell and not sure how he ended up on his ass. Kept telling the police that one of them had done it."

"I bet that went over well." Dean told him that they just stood him up, dusted him off, and warned him not to come around anymore. "Where are you guys staying while in town?"

Dean looked at Oakley, and Sheppard had a feeling that he wasn't going to like the answer. Or they were afraid of telling him. He asked what was going on. Dean spoke first.

"About two years ago I had a house put on the back part

7

of the farm. It's a nice house, fits me well enough. I could have gone all out, but I didn't want to." Sheppard looked at Oakley as Dean continued. "He has a house too, but a mite bigger than mine. Nothing too big, mind you, but like I said, it suits. The other three have been doing the same thing."

"Did you think I'd be pissed off or something? Why didn't anyone tell me? It's been two years, you said." Dean leaned back and just looked at him. "Look. I'm exhausted, dirty, and I've not been on the grounds but a few times in the last sixteen years. Tell me or don't—I don't have it in me to care what you guys are doing out there."

"Ma signed the land off to the six of us. She did that about a month after she decided that she liked where she was staying. You did good with that, Sheppard. Ma surely did like it there." He thanked Oakley. "Grandda, he's not been in a good way since Grandma died. I know that it's been a while, but you'd think that it was just yesterday. We've none of us told him about Ma dying yet. Dad complained that he had to take him out there every day for the last few months so he can sit with Grandma. It's not doing Grandda a lick of good, but you know how stubborn he can be."

Sheppard did know how stubborn the old man could be. He was chasing the tail of being ninety years old, and having a good time with life—before Grandma had passed away, anyway. Sheppard—Sheppard James Cartwright Marshall the fourth—was named after him. Several other grandfathers farther back, too. All of them stubborn, each of them living to be well past a hundred and having a good long life. Then there was his father. Not so much stubborn, but an ass, a thief, as well as a drunk. There wasn't much at all that could be said that was nice about his father. No one tried. Not even their ma had.

The cemetery was beautiful this time of year. The people that took care of it did a wonderful job of it. The trees were trimmed back. All the markers were upright and free of moss. Also, if there were plants put on any of the graves, they made sure they didn't get too big. His ma's parents had been buried out here, and that was why they'd made sure that she had a space next to them. Sheppard didn't know where his father was going to end up. None of them wanted him anywhere close to where Ma was.

After the service was over, the six of them decided to go into town and have some dinner. Sheppard had booked a hotel to stay in for the next week. He'd also rented a truck to drive around. He'd have to be careful of driving. It had been a while for that as well.

Shep, as they called him on the rigger that he worked on, had started out on the lowest rung of the ladder working an oil rig. It paid good now that he was higher up on the ladder, but he'd grown sick of doing the job of two people for the pay of only one. Especially when the other man was like his father in so many ways.

Hank Jones had been a drunk when they were on the same level. But through a great many lies being told and a great many asses being kissed, Hank had made it to the top level. That was ten years ago, but for the last several he'd been pushing his work off onto Shep. When the big bosses came around to see what was going on with the rigs, just their usual visits, Shep had heard Hank telling them all the ideas that he'd come up with. Every last one of them was Shep's.

The call about his ma had come about the time he'd been ready to tear the man a new ass. But he'd only had a couple of days at most to make it home in time for her funeral. Shep had made it without any time to spare.

On the plane home he'd put in his resignation. It was that or be fired for throwing his boss off the rig into shark infested waters. He wasn't even sure that the sharks would have eaten the man. They'd be drunk after just one bite.

He spent a good evening with his brothers. The six of them had been on their own for a long time, but they'd taken good care of their ma, sending money to her when she needed it, and even when she didn't. Even though Shep was far away out in the middle of the ocean, he remembered to send her flowers and chocolates not only on her birthday, but Mother's Day as well. Even when there wasn't any sort of holiday he'd send her some, just because he loved her.

His phone was ringing as soon as he got out of the elevator. Not answering it, he made his way to his room at the hotel and opened his door. Shep had dropped off his luggage at the front desk, and they'd assured him that they'd take care of it for him. They had.

The first order of business was to get a shower. Just standing under the hot water felt like he'd gone to heaven. Washing his hair three times, he even used the little bottle of conditioner too, just because he could. By the time he dried off, Shep didn't have enough energy to pull the blankets down, but fell onto the bed and was out before he could turn off his phone.

The ringing phone woke him and Shep reached for it. "This had fucking better be important, or so help me, I'll hunt you down and tear you apart." He felt his cat roll over him when he heard sobbing at the other end of the phone. "Who is this?"

"Sally. You didn't call me." He didn't know any Sally. He started to tell her that when she started talking again. "You got out of prison and you didn't call me. After all I did for you, you just left me in the dirt."

"I don't know who you're calling, but I don't know you. I've never been in prison either." She asked him who it was. "I just told you I don't know you. Why don't you hang up and try again?"

"He left me hanging." Shep wasn't going to get into this with anyone, especially someone that he didn't know. "Did you hear me?"

"I did. And now that you've woken me up from the first good sleep I've had in a while, I'm going to hang up. Lady, take my advice. Let him leave you hanging. You don't want to get mixed up with some guy from prison." She started cursing at him and he simply hung up. He didn't have time for this shit.

Shep was wide awake now, so he got up and took another shower. He wanted to go to the house and run for a few hours. Being on a rig didn't afford him much time to run as his jaguar, much less shift when he needed it.

Driving out to the farm, he was surprised to see Trenton there. He said that he was working on getting some of the things in the house fixed up. Shep, having nothing but time on his hands now, said that he'd help after he had himself a good run. Trenton decided to join him, and they stripped down and took off.

It had been too many years since he'd felt this free, Shep thought. Much too long, too, since he'd fixed something that didn't leave oil running in his eyes. He might even ask if any of them cared if he stayed in the family house for a while. He could work on it and figure out what he wanted to do with himself.

~*~

Sheppard heard her coming before she got where he could see her. Harrison Parker. He would never tell anyone, but he was kind of sweet on her—like a man to a daughter, that was. She stopped for a minute and shook her head before speaking to him. It was usually something snide and full of curse words, but he thought he liked that about her. She didn't care who he was.

"You know that your wife has been gone for nearly fifteen years, right?" He said he missed her every day. "Yeah, I can see that. Yet here you sit, pining away for a woman that can no more offer you comfort than the stone that marks her passing. What do you plan to do, Mr. Marshall, sit here until they find your body all crippled up from sitting on that bench? Or a human popsicle that kids eat all day? Doesn't sound to me like anything that wife of yours would have wanted."

"Now see here. You can't talk to me that way. I had a good life. One that I miss with her." Harrison nodded. "I don't think I want you coming around me anymore. You're not nice at all. And here I was thinking that I liked you a bit. Well, I've changed my mind."

"Suit yourself, sir. But you told me that you have a beautiful daughter-in-law that you love like your own child. Six grandsons that you've had a part of raising. And a son... well, we won't go into how you feel about him. I don't know how you could be here, with the dead, when you have so much life at your fingertips." He told her to mind her own business. "Yes, I can see that you're as stubborn as all men are. I have to tell you, Mr. Marshall, you certainly are about the most stubborn man that I've ever met."

"I'm doing what I need to do to get by. What about you?" She didn't answer him. Harrison usually didn't when it was about her. He'd already figured out she was military, but what she was, he wasn't sure. "You got you a family at home that you have pining away for you?"

"Let me ask you something, Mr. Marshall. What do you want your grandkids to say about you? Is it that Grandda is finally with Grandma? Or do you want them to say 'Grandda, he sure was a pistol, and I'm glad he knew how to have a good time.'" He looked at her. "Up to you. But I'd think that with six grandsons, you'd be able to find one or two of them to get into trouble with."

"And what about you? You run this path day after day. Who you out having fun with, young lady?" James, his worthless son, came out of the car whining about how long he was taking, and Sheppard waved him off. "You got someone out there who is going to say, 'Gee, Harrison wasn't one to hang out with.'"

"They're all dead." She stretched her legs again, and he knew she was about ready to take off. "Mr. Marshall, I'm going out again in the morning. I don't know each time I go if I'll be back. But I swear to Christ, if I come home and you're still sitting here day after day, I'm going to roll you over into a hole on the other side of your lovely wife and bury you. Understand? Because the way I see it right now, you're already playing dead."

When she jogged off, he sat there for a few more moments. Sheppard looked at his wife's marker, and realized that Harrison was right. He was playing dead. And he was going to do something about it right now.

Walking to the car wasn't difficult, but the ground wasn't as smooth as a floor. When he leaned against the car, James beeped the horn at him, nearly scaring him right into that grave Harrison was talking to him about. Flipping his son off, he was glad to see that he'd been able to shock him a little. As soon as he got in and buckled up, James started talking at him. Never to him, he just realized, but at him.

"I'm going to need this car for a few days." Sheppard said no, he had plans for it. "What are you going to do, old man? Drive it into a tree? I said I needed it, and you're going to sit over there and not say shit about it when I drop you off at the nursing home."

"You take my car, James, and I'll call the police and say that you stole it off me. They'll believe me too, since you've done it before." The car stopped so suddenly that he was glad for his belt over him. "You trying to kill me?"

"Yes, as a matter of fact, I am. I told you not to argue with me. Now, get your skinny ass out of this car and leave me to it."

Sheppard got out but he didn't go far. Calling the police gave him the most satisfaction he'd gotten in some time. As soon as his son turned the corner after leaving him beside the road, Sheppard heard the sirens. That felt pretty good too.

As soon as the officer brought him back his car, Sheppard showed him that he surely did have a license to drive, and he'd had nary an accident in nearly fifty years. By his estimation, that was about double how long the boy had been around. Getting in his car, he noticed that his boy had left behind his wallet and a few other things. Tossing them to the back seat where his son had been tossing trash for a while, Sheppard smiled. It was time to get with the living.

Since he'd checked himself into the nursing home, the quality care place that he was in, he had no trouble checking himself out. Gathering up a big trash bag, he cleaned out his back seat and the floorboard, and put the wallet and notebook that James had under the seat. Not a clue what was in it, he thought he might take it by to him before he left. Then he set to packing his things.

It was not that he hated the home he was in. They had all right food. The nurses were young little things that sure made a man smile. And it was a roof over his head. There was big enough yard out back with some trees where he could go out in the middle of the night and have a good run. As a jaguar, he figured that was why he'd been in such good health all these years.

Packing was a little harder than he thought it would be. Not that he owned a thing that was heavy, but the memories would flood him so badly that he'd have to sit a spell and think on things. The quilt that laid on the bed when he and his Millie had been married. There was the blanket that she'd made just for sitting that he used in the rocker in his room. Even the shirts that he had, most of them as checkered as his son's past, were soft as cotton and warm as toast.

His Millie had gotten him one for every birthday and Christmas. He'd teased her once that he had enough to open himself a department store. She didn't stop buying them, and he didn't care. It was wonderful to have a new one twice a year, and to know that she'd picked them out just for him. Sheppard missed that too.

By the time he was finished packing up, he needed some food. Sheppard loved drive thru shopping, and got himself a big burger and a milk shake to go. Getting on the road, he thought about Harrison. He'd have to figure out how to tell her that he'd moved on, and remembered that she'd given him her number. Just in case. The thing went to voice mail when it connected.

"Going to live with my pretty daughter-in-law and them grandboys of mine. Isn't far from where I was staying, but you can find me. The name of the farm is Marshall's Shadow. You come out for a visit sometime, and I'll have my Jill Ann make you a fine meal for visiting me." The thing beeped that he was done before he could think of anything else to say, so he pulled back onto the road, from the side where he'd stopped to make the call, and drove the few miles to the farmhouse. He was looking forward to staying there with the boys and Jill Ann. Yes, he thought, that was what he'd needed. A good talking to by someone that was strong enough to do it.

Pulling up in front of the big farmhouse, he could see that someone was doing some work on the place. There were roofing supplies there on the ground, some other things in boxes that he'd have to check out, as well as a ladder leaning against the house by the upper floor.

Getting out, two men came around the side of the house, and Sheppard was embarrassed to say that it took him too long to recognize that it was his grandboys. If he didn't miss his bet, it was Shep and Heath. Both of them hugged him up like he'd been gone forever.

"Grandda, you still have that old caddy, I see." He hugged Shep again when he commented on his car. "You staying? I've only just got the kitchen fixed up, and it'll be nice having some company."

"Where is that momma of yours? Her cherry pie is all I could think about all the way here. We should make some homemade ice cream too." When they didn't laugh with him, Sheppard just knew that she'd gone and left him. "No. Please tell me that she's not gone too. Why didn't anyone tell me?"

"You didn't seem to be in a place that made us feel like you'd take it well." That was true enough, he thought, but they still should have said something. "She didn't want much, Grandda. Just a little service and no one there but family. We didn't even put it in the paper for fear of Dad coming along and making a scene."

He was taken into the house. Sheppard wasn't sure if he'd been carried or he'd walked on his own, but there he was sitting in the parlor with a blanket over his legs. He'd forgotten how chilly this room could be.

"She go fast, or did she have herself some trouble with it? I didn't even know she was sick, to tell you the truth." Heath said that she'd had a car accident, and that she'd died on the scene. "That woman never could drive. I loved her, you know. More than your daddy."

"She knew that too, Grandda. Ma talked to us about you daily. Even when you moved out there to that home, she thought of you daily." He nodded at Heath, telling him that was nice of him to say. "When we were cleaning out the freezer, we found some of her pies. If you're staying here tonight, we can thaw one out and have it with some steaks. Shep is living here for now. Maybe forever. He's not decided."

"You home for good, boy?" Shep nodded. "Good. A man should be where his roots are. I never cottoned to you being so far away, but I do know that you needed to stretch your wings a bit. Being out there on the water all the time, I'm betting you had to get your earth legs back under you."

"I did." They all three laughed and Heath said that he had

17

to go into town for a bit, but he'd bring back some steaks. Shep looked at him when he asked him if he was all right. "I'm not sure, Grandda. I've missed so much here. Not just the family, but everything. When I left here all those years ago, I had it in my head that it would only be for a little while. Then before I could think about it, nearly all my life was gone."

"Don't say that, Shep. You got a long life ahead of you." He nodded. "Something else is bothering you. You tell me what it is, and I'll tell you it isn't worth a hill of beans to be worrying over."

"I couldn't give Ma what she wanted." Sheppard didn't know what to say to that, so waited for his grandson to explain. "All she talked about was having a daughter-in-law to go shopping and such with. She said she needed to have a balance in some way. And a grandbaby. I didn't do any of those things."

"You think that is all she wanted out of you boys? To make you into breeding machines? Darn it, boy, she was as happy as a lark having you six around her all the time. I know for a fact that you protected her from that son of mine on more than one occasion. And it wasn't you having a wife and a child that would have made her happy; it was having you happy to have a family of your own." Shep said that they had all loved her. "Well, of course you did. She was a woman that you'd be hard pressed not to love. Jill Ann, she might have said she wanted those things from you, but you can be sure as rain making mud in the dirt that she was just as happy with you six being here with her and loving her."

"I did. We all did." Sheppard stood up and asked where he would be staying. "You're here for good? You're not going to be cramping my love life, are you, Grandda?"

18

"Just so long as you won't be cramping mine, you whippersnapper."

Shep helped him bring his things into the house. He started to put him in the master bedroom, but Sheppard didn't want it. He didn't think it would be right for some reason. But he was just down the hall, and that suited him just fine and dandy.

# Chapter 2

Harris moved into the house, keeping an eye out for someone that might want her dead. She supposed that there were a great many people that wanted her dead at the moment, but she didn't really care. She had a job to do, and she was going to do it.

Moving as silently as a mouse through the living room, she saw that the man that lived here was going to be a fat fuck. There were pizza boxes and fast food bags everywhere. There were times, like right now, that she'd like to just sit down and wait for the fucker to come back to his steaming pizza and kill him then. But there were rules, and she had to follow them. Most of the time anyway.

"We have heat in the room just to your left." The voice in her earphone spoke quietly too. "I think he's in the shower. The heat goes hot to hotter every few seconds."

Harris wouldn't answer him. Her voice would carry no matter what the circumstances were around her. Instead, she moved to her left and found that the voice had been right. The shower was running.

"Boss said to tell you to break his neck. I believe he thinks you're super woman or something." She nearly laughed, but caught herself. The kid, Tommy, whom she'd never met, was going to pay for that if anyone was listening in on the other end of their conversation. "Sorry. I'm a tad stressed right now."

Harris knew that he was. Everyone was. With the changes that were coming in her department, she wasn't sure if she'd have a job in a few weeks or not. It didn't matter to her one way or another. With her skills, she thought that she could get a job just about anywhere she wanted. Harris wondered if she could flip burgers for a while.

The water turned off and she slipped into the steam filled bathroom. He was a fat fuck, just as she'd known he'd be. And he couldn't carry a tune, either. His singing was so off key that she wanted to kill him just for fucking up the song she'd heard recently.

This man was on her list of people that had fucked up so badly that he needed to be taken out. It was her job to make sure that they didn't do the bad thing that they'd been doing any more. Harris laughed a little. That made it sound as if they'd stolen a candy bar, when in reality they'd been screwing the government in some heinous way.

He saw her just as she lifted her gun up. He glanced at the gun that was on the sink, too far away for him to get to easily, so Harris made a quick decision. Kill him like she'd been told.

There wasn't any way that she was going to get to break his neck by grabbing him, so she kicked his feet out from under him with her foot and watched him tumble into the tub and hit his head. That was it, he was dead.

Moving through the house, she was careful not to disturb anything else. Going to the basement in the house, she heard the voice in her head. He sounded slightly more stressed than before.

"I don't see a heat signature anywhere in the house but you. All the cameras have been turned off since you entered, so you have no worries on that part. There must be a short there or something. Also, along the streets surrounding the house for five miles." She didn't say anything as she went down to the lower levels with her gun still at her side. "I know you can't answer me, but I'd like to tell you that wherever you go after this, if we're shut down, I'll work with you. You're the best there is."

The cinder block cell had only a small opening. She supposed that it was for feeding the man she'd been sent to find. Taking the key off the ring next to the cell, she opened the huge steel door. The man there cried, and begged her not to hurt him again. Harris pulled out her badge and showed it to him. Nodding, he just stared at her for several minutes.

She was dressed in a body suit that made sure that only her eyes were showing. No DNA would be left behind when she left. Harris would not leave any prints because of the gloves she wore. And since she'd not had to use her gun, there would be no way that anyone would think that anyone had ever been in the house.

When he opened his mouth to speak, she put her finger up to her lips to tell him to be silent. He was more than cooperative, but too weak to move on his own. Helping him to stand, she put him over her shoulder and made her way out of the house and to the car on the next street over.

Harris ran and lifted weights daily just for this reason. It wasn't the first time that she'd had to carry out a person that she was to rescue. She thought of Mr. Sheppard as she put the man in the back seat and covered him up. The old man was going to live a good deal longer simply because she'd been having a shitty morning. Smiling, she realized that every day was a shitty one in her life.

After calling in that the cake was baked, the stupidest way she'd ever heard of telling them that the job was finished, she got the coordinates to meet the helicopter at the pad to transfer. Harris could cook, so long as it had microwave instructions on the box and it wasn't popcorn. Never in her life had she been able to make a thing of popcorn in the sucker without burning it to a nasty crisp. She had no idea why that popped into her head. It had nothing at all to do with calling in to get the body removed.

The transfer went smoothly, and she turned in the gun that they always gave her. Harris never only had one gun. If she had all these years, she'd have been dead a while back. Getting onto her bike, she pedaled her ass to her car to drive to the hotel. It had been a long week.

The television was off, and she was sitting at the table making notes when the hotel phone rang. She didn't even bother getting up to answer it, but did unplug it from the wall. It mattered little to her who knew she was here. Yesterday she'd taken a tour of the chapels here, and today she was going to go and look at the old cemeteries that had been on her list of things to do. Anyone would think she was a single woman going on a nice vacation.

The knock at her door, like the phone, went unanswered. She'd not ordered anything, and the sign on the door, Do Not Disturb, should have kept the staff away. Pulling her gun from its holster, she held it in her hand when the second knock came.

"Miss Smith? This is the desk clerk. There is an urgent phone call for you." She didn't speak, but did get up to look through the peephole. Of course, it was blacked out somehow. "It's a man by the name of Reynolds."

Unlocking the door, she stepped back and into the closet that was there. Just as soon as the door was opened, two shots shattered the window by her bed, as well as the lamp. Firing once, she killed the man that entered.

Harris didn't see anyone else, but that didn't mean shit. Sliding to the desk, she picked up her notebook as well as the pen she'd brought. The rest of the stuff in the room was window dressing. Nothing of concern, and no fingerprints in the room. She didn't have any to leave.

Snaking her way out into the hall, she saw that the man had been alone. The idiot hadn't even bothered to steal a uniform to hide who he was pretending to be. Pulling him into the room and locking the door behind her, she tried to think what to do now. Putting several towels under his head to catch the blood, she used one of the pillows to absorb more if he bled out.

Obviously she couldn't call her boss. Whoever sent this guy not only knew she was here, but that he'd have to be slick about getting in. And the only person who would have known that was her boss. Another clue to that was that he knew the name of the person that they used. Reynolds was a code name for her to know that they were from the company.

Harris thought about the three cameras she'd found in the room, as well as the two mikes. She should have been forewarned when she found them. Unbeknownst to anyone,

25

Harris had a special knack of finding all sorts of things like cameras and recording devices. It had saved her from having her face plastered all over the world.

Pulling out her cell, she saw that she had another message from Mr. Marshall, but didn't have time for it at the moment. Instead, she called Carol. Carol was the person that she had befriended who did amazing clean up jobs.

"Carol's Dry Cleaning. How may I help you?" Harris told her the number, then the name that she used with her. The number was one that they had established for her to work for her. "Where might I pick up your cleaning, miss?"

After giving her the name of the hotel, she heard the elevator ding. It might not bode well for her to stick around here. Harris was glad now that no one had this number but Carol and Mr. Marshall.

"I won't be here. Bill me." Carol said that she could do that, and asked what she was getting for her. "One. Head wound. I've done the best I could."

"All right." She gave her a time when she'd be there and said that she would get it done. "Thank you, miss. I look forward to working with you again."

After hanging up, Harris grabbed her large bag, put all her personals in it, the notebook, gun, and extra clips, and was out the door. Her big hat was perfect for covering her face, and the sunglasses were huge on her small face. Christ, this was a nightmare.

There was no one in the hallway when she stepped toward the elevator. Smiling at the two big beefy men that were in the elevator, she asked if it was raining yet. When neither answered, she rode down when they got off. Might be a bigger mess than she'd thought.

Harris had taken care that the company knew very little about her. They thought that her name was Cora Banks. If they were to pull up the file on her, they'd find nothing but blank paperwork. The picture would be of someone that she'd found in a new wallet. And there was no known address for her. Basically, like her, everything in her life was a front to them. Harris was little more than a ghost to anyone — with the exception of Mr. Marshall.

Pulling out her cell, she pretended to shop and talked to him on her phone. He told her where he was living and what he'd been doing since staying there. Then he said that his girl, Jill Ann, had been killed. Her heart broke for the elderly man. He really had loved her very much.

Snaking her way in and out of shops, she didn't think she was being followed. Taking off the sweater that she had on and pulling on a hoodie, she put her things into her bag. The hat came off with her wig, and she moved to a few more places. Things were getting out of hand, and she was afraid for the first time in a very long time.

Harris needed a place to hide. The only person in the world that came to mind was Mr. Marshall. But she didn't want to bring trouble down on his grandchildren's heads, so she had to think of something else.

Just as she moved into one of the many stalls that were along the alley where she was, a pain in her left side alerted her to trouble. Whoever was out for her wanted her dead. Moving to the next stall where Tamara, a contact and a good friend of hers, worked, Harris slipped under the counter where Tamara hid her, and tried to collect her thoughts. As she laid there thinking, a first aid kit was tossed at her and she tried to move around to take care of it.

"They have gone by. What have you gotten yourself into today?" Harris only smiled at Tamara. "No telling, huh? You're not bleeding badly, so turn and I will fix it for you." Tamara had taught her French, and in turn, Harris had taught her how to speak English. Neither of them were good at it yet, but their friendship had grown a great deal. "Gone through, so you should be fine if I stitch you up."

"I need to get out of here. They might be able to figure out where I am, and I don't want to get you into trouble."

Tamara just huffed at her as she sprayed something on her skin to freeze the wound. As soon as she felt the needle enter her flesh, she tried to think of anything but what had just happened to her.

~*~

Shep was just falling asleep when the phone rang. He'd forgotten that he had it turned on, and when it rang a second time, he was sure that someone was going to pay dearly for making him get up to answer it. Barking out his name, he waited for the person on the other end to either speak or hang up. He was hoping for the other. Then a woman speaking French started talking quickly.

"*Je suis vraiment désolé. Je dois avoir le mauvais numéro. C'est celui qu'ils m'ont donné. Je suis désolé.*" Shep could speak French, but she was speaking too quickly. He asked her to slow down in the same tongue. "English? Do you speak English?"

"Yes. Better than I do French. I know that you said you were sorry, but after that, I got a little lost." She told him what she had said. "You might well have the wrong number, but let us start again. Who are you? And who is it you're looking for?"

"His name is Sheppard Marshall. She said he was an

elderly man. Do you know him? I heard your name is the same last, but not the first." He asked her what she wanted with him. "Ah, yes. She, Harris, is harmed, and is being chased to kill, she thinks. Now she is fevered badly, and might need more than I can give to her."

Grandda came into the hall where he was and asked what was going on. Handing the phone to him, not really sure he wanted to get between Grandda and another woman, he stood there waiting while he talked to the other woman.

Grandda could speak French better than he could, so the conversation was completed in that language. It took him several minutes to figure out what was going on, but apparently Grandda had agreed to go and get this other woman and keep her safe. Before he could go back to his room to get ready to do, Shep stopped him.

"What do you think you're doing?" His tone, Shep knew, was too rude for the elderly man as soon as his grandda cocked a brow at him. "What I mean is, this woman is going to be killed, and you along with her if you go there and get her."

"She's my friend. And the only reason that I'm not sitting by your grandma's grave right now, dead as she is." Shep didn't know what to say about that, so didn't open his mouth. "I'm going to go and get her whether you like it or not. Now, you go back to bed. I'm a grown man, and I can certainly take care of a little woman."

"I'm going with you." Again the brow, but Shep chose to ignore it this time. "It's the middle of the night. You are a ninety-year-old man, and I'm going to go with you. One of us should be able to see beyond the next strip on the road."

"You keep it up and I'm going to go and do just what

29

Harrison told me to do. I don't have to listen to you harping on me like my son does when I want to go and visit my lovely wife's grave." Now he was nose to nose with his grandda. Shep had never seen him so angry before. "I told you, she's my friend, and I am going to go and take care of her. If I have to, I'll buy me my own house and make sure that I don't come around anymore."

Grandda started away and Shep stopped him. "Grandda. I'm sorry for talking to you that way and for treating you horribly. If you don't mind, please, I'd like to go with you just to make sure that she doesn't need someone to help her with something more. I don't know what it might be, but I want to make sure that you're all right too."

"All right. But you keep your comments to yourself and your mouth shut from now on. Unless you have something helpful to say, keep your tongue from wagging where it isn't needed." He said that he would. "Good. I'm leaving here as soon as I get dressed. No need for packing. She's only in the next county over. Won't take but an hour to get there and get back."

Shep grumbled, but he didn't do it in the hall. Going to his bedroom, he pulled on his dirty jeans and a clean T-shirt. Today he had planned to do laundry. Now he was going to be driving all over the state with his grandda. He supposed there were worse ways to spend the day, and went to the kitchen to get a bowl of cereal.

Just as he was about to pour milk over his cereal, Grandda joined him in the big room and said they'd get breakfast on the way, Shep bit his tongue while he put everything back. This was going to be a hell of a trip; he just knew it.

The trip wasn't that long, and he did get what he wanted

for breakfast. Shep loved those breakfast sandwiches, and had six of them before they got to the little burb where the woman was supposed to be. He wasn't sure what to expect from this job, but he wouldn't leave his grandda in the hands of someone that he didn't know.

Of course, his grandda had been taking care of himself for some time now. He'd not been around to take care of anyone, so he supposed he was making up for lost time. Grandda interrupted his thoughts when he told him to turn into a large downtrodden apartment complex.

"You're sure this is the right place? It looks abandoned." Grandda just stared at the large building. Some of the windows were card boarded up. Others had large, what looked to him like blankets over the glass. An air conditioning unit, one of the window kinds, was hanging out of one of the rooms by the cord. He could see too that the parking lot hadn't been taken care of in some time, as the grass in the cracks was as tall as the half of a car sitting in it. All the wheels were gone, and the hood of it was open wide.

"I don't know, son. I really don't. But this is where she told me to go." A woman came out of one of the yawning openings that had broken stairs in it. She nodded to them, waving them toward her. "I hate to say this, but I'm kind of leery of going there by myself now. Will you go with me?"

"Yes." He didn't tell him as they were getting out of the car that Shep was following him through this entire adventure. As soon as the woman was close enough for them to speak to, she spoke to them both in broken English.

"She is sick. Unwell." Grandda asked her name. "Tamara Jones. I have been friends with Harris for many years. She saved my life. You are Sheppard Marshall. You lie by your

31

wives grave and wish to join her. I didn't understand that part, but that is what she said to tell you. She died some time ago. Harris, she told me, but it was garbled and I could not understand her well enough. She is sick."

He got that she was sick, but what had caused it? While they were jaguars, getting sick from something wasn't possible for them. But if she had been poisoned, he wanted to know with what and how. Shep suggested calling the police.

"If you do, she said that she would like for you to kill her first." Tamara turned and made her way up the stairs in front of them. "I don't know what she does, but she is very good at it. Has money to spare, she told me. Once when I was being chased by my husband, she said that she'd take care of him. I have had no troubles since."

"She killed him?" He felt embarrassed at how loud he'd asked the question. "Are you telling me that she killed him?"

"Non. She only had him arrested, and he is in prison forever. You have a very ill mind, too. Harris does. Thinks no one is a good person—except for Sheppard Marshall. She said he is the best there is." The room they entered from the hallway was so different than the building it was housed in that he wasn't sure what turn they'd made to come here. "You like? I make all but the furniture. I love color."

"It's beautiful."

Grandda was right. It was beyond anything that Shep had ever seen before. Not only was it colorful, but it had been tastefully done. While the one individual color might have been too bright, it was tempered with something softer, a neutral color that would calm it somehow.

The bedroom was all neutral colors. He'd bet so that she could sleep better. Tamara had an eye for what she was doing, and he was thinking that she needed a larger outlet than her home. Shep decided he'd talk to her as soon as this was settled.

"She looks horrible. Do you know what's wrong?" Shep looked at the woman on the bed when his grandda spoke. She did look awful, sweaty and pale. Her hair was soaked throughout, which made it look like it could be a dark brown to a red coloring. "You said she was shot. Can you show that to me?"

Shep thought that he needed to pay more attention. Each time that he'd tune in, so to speak, he knew that he'd missed gaps of conversation. He didn't know when Tamara had told him that this Harris had been shot, but she had been. The wound, he'd bet, was causing her to be ill too.

"It's infected. I'd say that when it was stitched up, something was already in there and that sealed it in. Or there was something on the bullet. Do you have it?" Tamara took it from her nightstand and handed it to him. Shep looked it over before smelling it. "It's this. There is a poison on it that has left itself in her body. It looks like it hit a wall. Did it go through her?"

"It did. Harris told me to pull it from the wall. I had to search for some time to find it for her. You must be careful when you touch her, sir. She is armed. I cannot get the knife and gun from her."

Shep pulled back, as he'd started to touch the young woman, but it was too late. He was pulled to the floor with his arm behind his back. Shep hadn't seen her move, nor had he sensed that she was even awake. As he laid there, trying his best not to beg to be let go, the scent of blood nearly had him shifting. It was then that he felt what he could only assume

33

was a gun grinding its way into the back of his head.

"Who the fuck are you?" He said his name. "You're not Sheppard. I know him. Once more, fuck wad, who the fuck are you?"

"Honey?" He heard his grandda talking softly to the woman. "Harrison, honey, that's my grandson. We've come here to save you."

"He's a man, Mr. Marshall. You indicated that he was a little boy when we spoke." He told her that he would always think of them as little boys. "I'm in trouble. You're the only one I could think of to fix me."

"Fix you how?" The smell of blood was getting stronger, and Shep wanted to get up and see to the woman. "How did you expect my grandda to fix this for you?"

"Kill me."

The gun fell to the floor where he was. Shep didn't touch it for fear that she'd put something else in the back of his head—a knife or something to kill him. Instead, he sat up on his knees and looked down at her.

"She wants me to kill her, Shep. I can no more do that than I could one of you boys." He was glad to hear that and told him so. "What do I do now? I can't just leave her here. Whoever is after her, they might well come here and kill both of these pretty women."

"Let me think a moment." He calculated things in his head. That was what made him the man he was today—or had been. Shep could zip right through a scenario and see where things might have to be tweaked, changed completely, or even ditched. He looked at Tamara. "Is there anything here that you need? That you cannot live without?"

"You mean, I'm going too?" Shep nodded. Tamara looked

around. "Not that I can't replace, no. My cash, of course. But nothing that I was planning on taking with me when the building went down."

"All right. Gather some clothing for you to wear. Pretend that this is your last day and you have to bug out quickly." She started moving around the room, opening and closing the drawers of various dressers. Shep looked at his grandda. "We're going to need something bigger than that little car that I have now. Can you — ? Let me think again. No. I'll go and get me something larger. An SUV, I think. Will you three be all right while I'm gone? I'll get more medical supplies while I'm at it. Also, tell one of the boys to have Rodney on site when we get there. He's not practicing anymore, but he can help us out with this. Don't make any more calls."

He didn't have any idea what was going on, but he somehow knew that if there was anyone looking for her, they'd be trying all the tricks he'd seen on the television late at night. Shep didn't watch anything but crime television shows. Hopefully he wasn't making that many mistakes.

The dealerships around the area were huge and plentiful. He was careful of what sort of questions he asked the salespeople, but in his head he was figuring if there would be enough room for a woman to be laid out and worked on. Besides the driver and passenger, two more people too. Shep decided that instead of a smaller SUV, he would get a larger one, and also the four-wheel drive. Just in case, he told himself, they were chased.

After the price was set, he asked them if he could trade in his car. That was the way his mom had always done it — get a set price then dicker with them. He'd only just purchased the car, and was glad that he'd been able to pay cash for it. Things were suddenly looking up.

Driving the larger vehicle, he had to be extra careful. Not only was it longer and wider, but it was also higher off the ground. Driving to the drug store, he tried to think what he might need from there.

More than a first aid kit, he thought. Something more like a survival kit. He was looking at those when a man came up behind him, probably to see if he needed help. Alarms went off in his head when he noticed that the man wasn't wearing a name tag, nor did he have on the red shirt that the other employees had on.

"Boy, that's a huge kit for just starting out, don't you think? Do you like them big?" He didn't answer the man, but Shep felt his cat move along his skin. Then someone touched his mind. "I like them big too. And firm. They have to be firm."

*I don't know how the fuck I can do this, but do me a favor — look the man straight in the eyes for me.* He asked who this was. *Harrison Parker. I know your grandda. You're Sheppard too. That's why, I'm assuming, I can reach out to you.*

He turned and looked the man in the eye. The woman, Harrison, laughed before she spoke, then told Shep to tell the kid that he had this, and to go away.

*He likes big men.* Harrison laughed again. *I don't mean like big men that have an ego to match their head, which I think you have. Nor do I mean that you lift weights, though I guess you might, if Kelly there is on your ass. That's what he wants, big boy, your —*

*I understand what you mean, damn it.* He had to hide a smile from Kelly before sternly telling him to go away. When he did, Shep picked up the kit that he thought would be the best to help him see to the girl. *How can you speak to me like this? When I left you were barely conscious.*

36

*I don't know. I can hear voices around me. Tamara and Mr.
Marshall. Who, by the way, should have had one of you grown
assed men helping him out instead of letting him waste his life away
sitting by a cold grave all the time. And that son, I'm assuming
your father, needs to be strangled with his own tongue.* He asked
her if she was normally this violent as he paid cash for the kit.
*Yes, as a matter of fact, I am. By the way, I don't fucking know how
I'm doing this either, but not only are all the recording devices not
working wherever you go, but I have a feeling if asked, no one will
remember either your face or selling one of the kits you purchased.
That's a trick that I figured out when I was younger. Nothing will
record my face. Not even a camera on a phone. It's not like — Why
do you care, right? Okay, I'm starting to feel worse, so do you think
you can hurry your ass along? I need something now.*

All Shep could think about as he drove around the back
of the apartment building where Tamara lived was that
Harrison was certainly violent. As he was driving back, she
told him what else she was able to do, like see what he was
seeing when she concentrated on him. Getting out of his new
vehicle, he saw two used needles on the ground, as well as
several used condoms. No wonder they were tearing this
place down. It was a haven of shit like that, he'd bet.

# Chapter 3

Harris woke up in the biggest fucking bed she'd ever seen in her life. It had to be five feet across and at least nine feet long. The room, along with the bed, seemed to be clean and well taken care of, even if it was a little old.

"It was my wife's and mine when we were living here." Harris looked at Mr. Sheppard when he spoke. "I did what you told me, and darned if you didn't go and get yourself hurt anyway. What did you do, girl? Make some boss of yours angry?"

"I think I did in some way." He'd only been kidding, but she wasn't. Someone had a burr up their ass, and she was their target. "Are you going to be all right with me being here? Because I'm assuming that I'm not in a hotel, nor in the rat hole that Tamara lived in."

"No. My grandson and I—you met him, Shep—are sharing digs right now. This is the house that he grew up in. I raised his father here too, but he doesn't have so many good memories of the place. My Jill Ann, she was a pistol, she was.

I think you and her would have gotten along just fine." He laughed, then sobered up quickly. "You need to answer me a few questions, Harrison. Then I can tell you what we've done to make you safe here."

"Unless you hired an army to surround this place that are to shoot when they see their eyes, then there isn't any way that I'm all that safe. I work for—worked for some pretty high on the food chain people, Mr. Marshall." He told her to call him Sheppard. "Doesn't that get a tad confusing to you guys? All of you named the same name, I mean?"

"My son, the worthless piece of shit, goes by James." She paid attention to his body movements when he cursed. She'd never heard him do that before. "I go by Sheppard. My grandson—who is the fourth, by the way—goes by Shep. I don't know many that call him Sheppard. Or you could just call me Grandda. I think I'd like that."

"Anyone ever fall for your sweet little old man tricks?" He laughed and said that he'd never had much of an occasion to use them. "Yes, well, it's like you're pulling out all stops right now. How about I think on that?"

"You do that. All right, my first question. What branch of the service do you work for? If you can tell me." She stared at him, and wondered what he thought he might have figured out. "I'm assuming that it's for something, because of the way you think on your feet."

"That's why I'm good on my feet. I don't have a name. The branch I worked for only reported to two men." He nodded as if he understood. "If your next question is what is it I do, then you'd better be prepared for the answer, Mr. Marshall. I'm not what you'd think of as a person you might have a fun date with."

"I don't date. I'm assuming that you kill for these two men. And the two men don't include the president, though I suppose that he might have an inkling as to who you might be. Perhaps not your name, but— I'm even betting that the people you work for, they don't know the real name like I do, do they?" She shook her head. "Do I? Know your true name?"

"Yes. I'm Harrison Elizabeth Parker. I'm twenty-seven years old, and I've been a—what some might call a hit man, for the last ten years. Just about the time I got out of college." He asked her how old she'd been when that happened. "I was fifteen. But I didn't get out the nice and normal way, with good grades and on an honor system. I got out because I read a great many books all the time, and could remember what was in them as well as what page number it was on. I cheated."

"No, you used the talents that you had with you. That's not cheating, Harrison, that's using your noodle." She didn't comment. Harris knew what she'd done. "All right, those questions are sort of answered. Now, I must tell you a few things."

"Someone has given me something to combat the drug that was in my system." He nodded. "This someone, it's more than likely your grandson that I met. Shep."

"Yes, he was the only one that could have saved you, being the oldest son of the oldest, and so far back I can't remember. The line should have been broken when I only had the one child. Shep has...I guess you could call it a great deal of whatever was left behind that his father didn't get. Him not being the seventh of anything, only in line for brains." She laughed. Then she told him what she could do. "You trust me. Would you like to know why?"

41

"No, I would not. Not now, at any rate. Where is Tamara?" Mr. Marshall laughed. She wanted to call him Sheppard, but something inside of her, in her heart, also wanted to call him Grandda. He told her she was out with Shep. "Good. She doesn't date much, I don't think. Not since her husband was found out to be such a shit hole."

Mr. Marshall said that he had to run to get him a drink of something. He didn't drink coffee, so she figured that he was giving her time to get dressed. Sheppard was a wonderful man, and she was sort of sweet on him.

Harris started to stand, but felt slightly lightheaded. Holding onto the foot of the bed, she made her way to the bathroom. It was time to scrub up and get a handle on what the fuck was going on. The small knock at the door had her reaching for her gun, but it wasn't where she needed it to be. Someone had taken it. Harris would have to get it back, and soon.

"It's Grandda. See how that just rolled off my tongue? Anyway, there are clothes in the bottom of the linen closet for you to wear. Tamara picked them out for you." Harris found them right where he said they'd be. She asked him about her gun. "It's in the top of the same cabinet between towels. I don't know why Shep put it in there for you, but he's not been around guns all that much. Not like you have. The knife is there too, but wrapped in a washcloth. Your cell phone is in the safe downstairs. Shep got to thinking that it might have a tracker on it, and we put it in there for safekeeping."

Turning on the water when she was able to get all her things gathered up, Harris tried to think what was the last thing that was said to her about the job she'd done. She did worry about how much Mr. Marshall had been able to figure

42

out, but knew him to be a smart man. The touch to her mind nearly had her screaming out loud.

*You've been told about me giving you my blood by now. Are you all right?* Well, that settled one of the many questions that she'd had. It hadn't been drugs like she'd been thinking, but the man's blood. It occurred to her that she didn't know what he was. *I asked if you're all right.*

*Yes. I was thinking about what sort of shifter you are. And in answer to your question, no, I didn't know about the blood until you mentioned it. I think your grandda is working up to things slowly for some reason.* Harris could hear his frustration. *What are you doing that has you pissy like a bear in a trap? Your date with Tamara not going well? Don't hurt her, or I'll kill you.*

*Just as simple as that? You'll just kill me? No suffering? Nothing like stringing me up so that I hang upside down while you beat me? You're just going to kill me?* She washed her hair, thinking about the man that had given her his blood as he prattled on. *We're not on a date. I wanted her to look at some buildings in the downtown area for her to start up a new place to sell her wears. And before your mind leaps there, not her body, but the things that she makes.*

*Okay, first, my mind rarely if ever goes directly to sex. Secondly — well, this should have been first, but yes, I'd simply kill you. There is no reason for people to prolong the inevitable when it comes to ending a life. In my line of work, the faster the better. There is no talking to the person. No telling him why you're killing him. Trust me, when I go after someone, they know why I'm there and what's about to happen. Just plug one into his head or however I do it, and go on with my work. Too much hanging around can get your ass extinguished if you're not careful.* She felt his shock, almost like he was facing her, and she could read it on his face. *What*

43

*now? Have I pissed you off for some reason?*

*No, not pissed me off. You really do kill people?* Rolling her eyes, she got out of the shower and noticed that not only was her tat gone, but the wound in her side was all but gone too. Just the tiniest of scars was there, like it was still working on taking care that it didn't mar her body. *What is it that has you so distracted that you can't keep up with a conversation?*

*I had a tat. I hated it, got it one night when I was feeling down on myself and was drunk. But the fucker is gone. Also, you might well not believe this, but I'm healed. There is no bruising anywhere on me that would tell someone that I'd been hurt. What the fuck are you?* He told her. *No, you're not just an ordinary jaguar. You're something more. Your grandda said you were descended from a seventh son of the same all the way back, until your father. Why are you so special that you have all the magic that is supposed to come to one?*

*We don't know. Can you please talk Tamara into going into business with me on this? I'm giving her an opportunity of a lifetime here. She's acting like I'm trying to steal everything that she has.* Not worried about the change in subject, Harris told him that was exactly what she was thinking. That Tamara didn't trust men with her welfare. *So how do you think I should proceed with this? She needs this. I think she's that good.*

*Then convince her of that.* She pulled on the rest of her clothing and made her way into the hall just as she saw another man coming out of a room down the hall. Slipping her gun out, she put it to the back of his head when he walked by her. The man started laughing, and she knew without being introduced that he was related to Mr. Marshall somehow. He had the same laugh. *I think I just tried to kill your brother. Do they all live in this house with you?*

*No, and don't be killing anyone. Please. My family is very dear to me, and I'd just as soon not kill you for killing them. Even if I could.* He was silent for a few moments. *That's my baby brother Dean. He said that he'd not even known you were in the house, but he's glad to know that you know how to take care of yourself. He's only twenty-three, so please don't kill him.*

*I wasn't planning on it, but what the hell does him only being twenty-three have to do with whether or not I kill him?* Shep said that he didn't know, but he didn't want him dead either way. *You have an illogical mind. I'm going to eat, then get going here.*

She closed him out. Harris wasn't sure how she'd done that, but it felt good getting in the last word with the larger than usual man.

Finding the kitchen, she could only stand and stare at the large warm room. It wasn't warm as in it was too hot—no, it was warm in a friendly sort of way. The way Harris felt when she was at Tamara's house when she came back from work. Comforting, she thought it might be called. The woman at the stove asked her, without turning, if she was hungry. Before she could answer, if the question was directed at her, Dean said that he could always eat.

They were seated at the table when Dean smiled at her. He was a flirt, she knew that, and more than likely got laid because of his good looks. He was a charmer, just like his grandda. Harris wondered for a moment why she'd never thought that about Shep. Like it really mattered, she thought.

"You've pissed off Shep." The woman at the stove hit him across the hand with her spatula. All he did was grin at her. "You've upset Shep. And while I think that's great, he wants me to tell you something."

"What on earth could he have to say to me? I'm finished

talking to the idiot. Did you know that he asked me not to kill you because of your age? What a moronic thing to say. What did he want?"

Dean told her. Dotty, the cook at the stove, dropped not only her spatula, but also the glass that she'd been bringing to the table.

"What do you fucking mean, he's my mate?"

# Chapter 4

Shep saw her waiting for him on the front porch of his... their home. He'd been out most of the day, mostly to avoid her killing him, but now that he had to come home, Shep hoped that the old saying about not being able to harm your mate was true. It hadn't been for his parents, but it might hold true for them.

Before he reached her, she began talking to him. "Do you have any idea what it is that I do for a living?" He said that it didn't matter to him. "Sure it doesn't. But when I have to get up in the middle of the night to run out and blow some fucker's head off, what are you going to say then? Oh, and by the way, I've talked to Tamara, and she said you need to give her a few weeks to think on working things out. So don't bother her."

"Okay, I can do that. I would hope that you'd be safe, but other than that, the fact that you'd be able to come home to me is more than I could have hoped for." She huffed and got up to pace. Shep sat where she'd been, his legs just worn out from all the walking on the dirt all day. "Is this going to take long? The reason I ask is, I'm hungry and exhausted. Plus, I'm not used to walking around all day where the floor beneath me isn't tempered by the ocean floor."

"You work on an oil rigger." He answered her anyway, even though it wasn't a question. "Which one, and I can tell you if you're going to be in business for that much longer."

"I don't work there any longer, but I worked for Cranes Digs. Stupid name, I know, but it was a place that could pay well and make me work hard for it. I don't like to be idle." She said she understood that, but did tell him that he'd have been out of work soon anyway. "You killed Crane?"

"Yes. Just before I was shot, too. He was dipping his dick into a great many men on the rig. Not to mention, he wasn't playing well with the men in charge of such things. Such as, he was selling off his oil to people that the government didn't approve of. But what got him into deep shit was kidnapping and holding one of the president's sons as his plaything, so they'd let him do his thing." Shep asked why they didn't just talk to him first. "They had. It didn't take, apparently. Were you one of his playboys?"

"No. You said that you killed him. Did you know that the newspaper says that he fell in the shower? How is that remotely possible if you put a bullet in his head?" She didn't speak, and he figured it out on his own. "You knocked him around and made it look that way."

"Something like that. The rig that you were on, it's been shut down permanently, after the government bought it for about a tenth of what it was really worth. You'll have to find yourself other means of supporting yourself, I guess. You might say that I know things." Apparently she did. More than

48

he did. "Why do you think that I'm your mate? You'll notice that I didn't say I am, but why do you think so?"

"You have a scent." She cocked a brow at him, much like his ma used to do when he'd been living at home. "You have this scent about you, a smell that calls to me. Also, when I gave you my blood, it didn't just heal you, but shared some of the traits that I have. I think I picked up a couple of yours too. What are you?"

"I happen to be just a plain human that has a super brain. Not that I use it all that often, but I have it." He asked her why she'd say something like that. "Because I should have killed you when I had the chance. But I didn't, so now I have to figure out a way for you to fall in the tub when you shower."

"You could take a shower with me, and that would solve both our problems." Harris told him that she didn't have any problems. "Sure you do, if you think that I'm going to be letting you stand outside my shower ready to do me in."

"You're an ass. Other than this scent thing, what else? I know a few shifters, and scent is something that they don't rely on. It's been fucked up before." He said his parents were a prime example of that. "I met him, your father. He's a dick."

"He is at that. Mostly he's the reason that I left here. Not because I had to work—none of us do. But to get away before I murdered him. My mother made me promise that I'd only come home when one or both of them were dead. She died first." Harris asked if his father had killed her. "Not that I'm aware of, no. It was an accident. Drunk fuck ran a red light and T-boned her on the driver's side. She was waiting to turn into the grocery store parking lot when it happened."

"I'm sorry for your loss. Mr. Marshall, he calls her his Jill Ann. He's told me some things about her." Shep knew this too. After figuring out what Harris was to him, he had had a long talk with his grandda. "I'm in deep shit here, Shep. I don't know who is after me or why. I have to be out of the public eye for a while. At least until I can figure this out."

"What do you need to do that? As I said, I don't have to work. I have more money than I can spend in a couple of lifetimes. You tell me what you need and I'll see about getting it for you. From there, we can figure out what we're going to do about each other." She said that there wasn't going to be an each other. "There has to be, Harris. I know you don't want to believe that, but if you have shifter friends, then you have been told why it's important to keep mates together."

Harris shook her head, and Shep stood up. Her backing away from him pissed his cat off, but they had to work at this slowly. She wasn't timid around him, and in thinking that, he knew that she could hurt them both badly if they took a single misstep. In any direction.

"You just don't get it, Shep. I could be shot at any time from anywhere." He looked around, seeing nothing, but knew that wasn't the point she'd been trying to make. "Damn it, don't you get it? In the crossfire, one of your family or you could be murdered by this. I don't want that to happen."

"I don't either. We should talk about this and get what you need to get things in gear for you. First things first. What is it you need to call or text message someone to get your answers?" Shep held onto his laughter when she stomped into the house. He didn't want to change a thing about her, but was excited for her to mold him into whatever she wanted. Shep was already half in love with the spicy woman.

She was at the kitchen table when he found her, filling out a list of things she was going to need. The number one item was a secure phone. He had no idea how to make that happen, so called up his brother Oakley.

Oakley was their go to man when they had computer issues, as well as when anything was wrong with their cars. He was very smart about both, naturally. He'd not taken any classes or done any kind of work before he'd been able to take apart and revamp their old computer at home. Just the other day Shep had seen him working on Trenton's car. It had just stopped running, he'd been told. In less time than it took Shep to figure out what he wanted for supper, not only was the car running, but Trenton said it was running better than it had before.

"I have to talk to your grandda. I think he might have a way for me to get some of this without it causing anyone to look in this direction." He asked her what Grandda might have that he didn't. "Friends."

Leaving the list behind, Harris went to talk to Grandda. Looking at it, Shep had no idea where to even begin on such a thing. Not only did it have secure network, but it also had things like a router that would bounce. There were many other things too, things that he was sure even Trenton might not have heard of.

When she came back she seemed stunned. Asking her what had happened, he started to worry about her when she just sat there. After a few minutes of that, before he could figure out if slapping her to get her attention was a good idea, she looked at him.

"Your grandda is well connected, did you know that?" Shep said he didn't, as a matter of fact. "I think you guys all need to gather around him and give him a good time. He's feeling stuffed."

"I don't understand. What do you mean, stuffed? Like he's full?" She shook her head and looked at her list. "I'm all for taking Grandda out. He's a lot of fun when he's with us boys. But you have to explain to me what you meant by him being stuffed."

"When I was a child, my parents were the kind of people that other parents envied. They were good to me. Of course, they traveled a great deal. Most of the time they'd take me with them. We had a good life. They made sure that I was well dressed, loved, and had what I needed. They loved each other and me. Coming home from a trip to someplace, Dad brought me back a bear. His name was Alexander. Anyway, when Mom came to tell me good night, on the last night that I saw her, I told her that when I got older and had my own home, I was going to keep her and Dad safe. Then when they passed away, I was going to stuff them like Alexander and put them on my couch. She laughed and said that she'd like that. Hugs and kisses from me all the time. I think your grandda is feeling like he's already been stuffed and put on the couch, but no one is hugging him anymore."

He didn't know what to say to that. Neither the story about her parents—the first time she'd mentioned them that he knew of—or the feelings on his Grandda. Instead of asking her more about her family, which he really wanted to, Shep asked her why she thought that of Grandda.

"I asked him if he knew anyone in office. Any office that I could contact. He did, and is calling her now. He told me, with tears in his eyes, that I made him feel useful. Like he was needed. Then he said that he must have stayed so long at the graveside that he'd turned into a nobody." That hurt Shep badly. Not the words, but that his grandda felt that way. "You boys, as he calls you, need to rally around him and make him feel like a functioning adult, or he's going to shrivel up and die on you. Then it will be too late."

"What happened to them? Your parents?" She picked up the pen she'd been using. Shep didn't think she was going to answer. "You don't have to tell me if it hurts you too badly."

"They're dead." He nodded, and figured that was going to be the end of it. "The man that killed them, he's dead as well. I killed him when I was sixteen. He took their lives because he thought that our home would give him something that he needed. Money."

Robbery came to mind, but she said no more as she bent over her notebook. Shep sat there for several moments, not really thinking of anything but watching her hand move over the page, when Grandda joined them. He looked as if he'd been crying.

"I called a friend of mine to tell her about your momma passing on. She said that she'd not heard about it." Shep told him how they'd decided not to put anything in the paper because of their father. "Yeah, I told her that. She knows your dad too. Anyway, she's coming for a visit tomorrow. I've not seen her in a while, but it'll be nice to have a long talk with her, I'm thinking. Like I said, she knew your momma, and in turn knew your grandma too."

"Grandda, how about we go out to dinner tonight? I mean all of us." Harris said that she had plans, which he'd figured that she would. "I'm going to call my brothers and see about getting all gussied up and going to have a nice steak dinner together. We've not done that in a long time."

"You'd want to have dinner with me?" Shep knew right then that they were going to do just what Harris had told him, to involve Grandda in more projects. "I'd sure like that, Shep. I would. And a steak sounds about right."

Reaching out to his brothers, he told them what Harris had said, then what Grandda had said. They all agreed that they'd break whatever plans they already had to make this dinner. They were also willing to dress up. As soon as he had the arrangements made, he thanked Harris.

"You helped me a great deal with this. I owe you." She snorted at him and he laughed. "You're not terribly friendly, are you? Poor me, your mate, pining after his mate like a sad kitten."

"I've never seen your cat." He asked her if she wanted to now. "I'm not sure. I mean, can you get into trouble just running around like a cat when there are others around? Humans. Like me?"

"No. You're my mate, first of all, and that's an exception to any of the laws we have. Secondly, we have a great deal of land between the six of us, and we run on all the places as freely as we want." He watched her put the pen back in the notebook, then put it in the big bag that she carried around with her all the time. "I will warn you that I'm a bigger cat than those at the zoo. All of us are. I'm larger because I'm the oldest. Grandda is larger too, but his is graying like he is."

She nodded and he took her hand into his. Shep would take any opportunity he could to touch her. Harris was very skittish about being touched, he noticed. Making a mental note to look up the tragedy that had befallen her, he took her outdoors.

He didn't waste any time in shifting. Shep knew that to strip down would make her uncomfortable, so he just did what came naturally to him. Letting his beast take him, he sat down when she did and crawled on his belly to get closer to her.

"You're very overwhelming, aren't you? I mean in your size. I know that you said that you'd be bigger, but I wasn't sure how much larger that would be." He was close enough to touch her now, so he put his paw on her leg. It never occurred to him how overwhelming he was until he saw her small leg under his much larger paw. "I'm sorry that I was short with you about my parents. I feel as if I can talk to you this way. Lord knows I've seen enough shrinks about it in my life. If you were to look them up, you'd only see a small part of what happened that night."

*Tell me, love.* She looked at him, her face full of anger and fear. He'd never seen the latter on her face, and it surprised him a bit. *Tell me what happened.*

~*~

Harris thought of the night that her mother had come to tell her goodnight. The last night that she'd seen either of her parents alive. They'd read part of *Moby Dick*. Her mom had had the most beautiful voice to listen to, Harris had always thought. Looking away from Shep, she started from there, the reading of the book.

"We'd read *Moby Dick* twice before. Before I could read, then after I was old enough to read some of it by myself. It was fun for us, just my mom and me. Then after I was tucked into my bed, my dad would come in, untuck me so that I could get up when I wanted, and then he'd read something funny. Usually the *Stinky Cheese Man*." He told her that he'd read both of the books. Nodding, she moved on from there. "They both had kissed me on the forehead. I had, as I usually did, rubbed it into my skin so that it would be a part of me. When

55

you're only six, you can think all kinds of strange things, I guess."

*You were very smart then.* She nodded, and told him that both her parents had been geniuses. *What did they do for a living? I'm assuming that they both worked?*

"Yes. Even though, like you, they didn't have to, they worked every day. My mom was a brain specialist. She did surgeries too, but her primary care was seeing what made the brain work the way it did. My dad was an engineer. He designed concept machinery for things like wheelchair lifts and such. Mostly. Cars and other designs too. We had a great deal of money even before they were born." She thought about telling him that she had a home and money too, but decided this was about the story. "The house was silent when I woke up. I think that is what woke me, the lack of sound. I usually had a fan on in my room year round, and it had turned off. Getting up, I thought about going to see where the trouble was, but went to my bathroom first."

She had on her favorite jammies. They were yellow with little pink hearts all over them. A shirt and a pair of shorts. No matter the weather, she had always worn shorts sets like that to bed. Harris had no idea why that had popped into her head, but she told Shep about it.

"I went into the bathroom and closed the door, but didn't lock it. It was eerily dark and quiet in there, and I couldn't see my hand in front of my face. I think that is the only thing that saved me." Harris leaned back on the step and thought about what had happened. "The man just opened the door and said my name softly. I knew it wasn't my father—this man was heavier. He also had a beard. I saw it when he turned his head to look at my bed. Even though I had only gotten up to go see my parents, I'd had the strangest idea that I needed to make my bed. I did before going into the darkened room to pee. I think that he thought me gone from the house. Unbeknownst to him, he had signed his own death warrant."

*You said that they robbed you. Was it only the one man, or were there more?* She told Shep that there had been two of them. *You killed the other man, didn't you?*

"Yes, but it was too late for me to save my parents." He said that she was just a child. "I know that. I knew that when I'd gotten the gun from my father's safe. I had had lessons on firing it, how to load it. I knew even then that someday I'd become very familiar with a gun, and that night was my first lesson in killing someone."

The gun had been so large in her small hand. It didn't seem to matter, she supposed, because so long as she'd been able to pull the trigger, then it was a perfect fit for her. Still not looking at Shep, she continued with her tale.

"The bedroom that they had was empty. There was blood on the sheets, but I tried not to think about how much was there. In hindsight I know that it was very little, but then, it seemed like someone had bled to death." Her mom's things were broken all over the room, along with her dad's. "They had searched the room for things. Some of her rings were gone. Her mother's watch too. Dad's things were in disarray, but I didn't know what they kept in there, so I had no idea if things were missing or not.

"Sneaking down the stairs, I was shocked to see that the living room looked as if someone had taken a knife to the cushions on the couch and chairs. The pictures on the mantel had been knocked off, the ones that my mom would change out every season as if that were part of her making the house ready for this event or that." Harris still had the pictures that had been knocked to the floor. "Mom had only put them up the week before. We had gone skiing, and they were from that trip. Lamps had been overturned. The paintings on the walls had been moved and torn to shreds. They were looking for a safe, I was told later. They never found what they were looking for."

*How long were they in your house?* She told him less than four hours. *You killed one of the men. Is that when it ended?*

"No. My parents were in the dining room. They had been beaten up and tied to the chairs. My dad saw me first. He didn't say anything, but he did look to his left, just a small movement that gave me a clue that the man or men were standing there. I didn't move for fear of doing something to alert them that I was there. My mom, she asked for a glass of water, please. I haven't any idea why, but I knew she was telling me that the other man was in the kitchen. I went there first." Harris knew that Shep would not want to be around her after this. Not that she wanted him around now. The man hadn't a clue what sort of person she was. "He was in the fridge when I found him, his body bent down so that he could see what was in it. It was a larger refrigerator than most had. A double wide that held all sorts of treasures, I guess. I put the gun at his ass and fired. Just like that."

*You wounded him.* She told Shep how the bullet had traveled up his ass and into his spine, then brain. She'd killed him. *Christ, what a wonderful shot. How did you know to do that?*

"I didn't. I only wanted to wound him, as you said, but it happened so quickly that I know that I was only reacting instead of thinking. Moving to the pantry, I slipped in there when the other man came into the room." She remembered the face of the man and would forever, she thought. "He found me easily enough and knocked me out. When I woke up, I was in a chair with my parents. They were both dead. He'd killed them after finding me with my father's own gun."

*I'm so sorry, Harrison. To be so young and to lose your parents that way. I just don't know how you did it.* She nodded but didn't speak yet. There was more to tell yet. *Honey?*

"I had called the police by tripping the alarm in the house after I shot his partner. They were en route. At least I hoped they were when he made me take the gun and put it to my own head. He, I guess, supposed that everyone would think that I'd killed my parents then myself when I realized what I'd done. I don't know what he was going to do about the man in the kitchen. Nor how that would explain why the house was trashed." He seemed to understand there was more to this. "In the ten minutes between me waking up and the police showing up, he asked me where the money was. Beat me until I couldn't move without hurting. My face was so swollen from his fists that it took several surgeries to put it back together. He'd broken my arm and hand, and screamed at me for killing his brother."

*You didn't tell him.* She told him that the safe had been in her bedroom. And that she'd not told him anything. *He would have killed you anyway.*

"Yes, he told me that, several times in those few minutes." Harris remembered his slurred words as his spit hit her in the face. The way he didn't pronounce words correctly. Like gun and blood — he'd called them gon and blad. She told Shep that. "It was something that the police ignored when I told them. Said that I'd misheard him, didn't take into account, they told me, that it was two in the morning and both my parents were dead. The DNA that he'd spit on my face was from his brother, the courts told me. A near enough match that they eventually blamed everything on Thomas and not Charles, who had killed my parents."

*So he was set free.* She nodded. *How did he get out of the house? I'm sure however he did, it's really going to piss me off.*

"It did me too, and I was only a kid. He heard the first sound of them coming and ran out the back door. I don't think it was ever explained by anyone how Thomas had been killed like he was. How I had shot him the way he'd been shot. Every time I tried to tell them it was me, they only patted me on the head and told me that I'd done well, for a kid." She could see that he was processing her story. It didn't matter to her if he believed her or not; she'd been the only one there that could tell it the way it really happened. "After he left us, the police came into the room. My mom had been shot once in the head. My dad had suffered more. His knees had been shot, then his wrists. The one to his head was just window dressing, I heard one of the officers say. He would have bled to death from the wrist wounds."

*You survived.* Harris told him that she had, barely. *And the legal system let you down by not convicting the right killer. That's why you went after him, to make it right.*

"Yes. My father taught me several things when he was alive. No one is perfect, and those that think they are more than likely are the most flawed of all. Everyone wants to seek revenge, but few do it. He told me that you might say that you don't want revenge. That it's not in your nature. But you need it. Not everyone gets it, but we all need to feel like we would have." Shep nodded. "He also taught me that nothing in life is free. Nothing. Not the breath that you take nor the beat of your heart. There is a price for it all. For those things, it's the ending of your life. And if you want something badly enough, you have to figure out a way to get it or it will haunt you for the rest of your life. 'I should have' and 'I wish I had' will not make you a happy person in the long run."

*I think I might have liked your dad. Your mom, she was someone that I bet you look like, don't you?* Harris told him that she could be her twin right now. *I'm so sorry for everything that you lost. In my opinion, you lost a great deal more than just your parents that day. You lost your childhood, the feeling of being safe, as well as a place that you could be safe in. I'm so sorry, Harrison.*

"I've never told anyone that story before." Shep asked if she felt better. "No. I feel everything all over again. But I'm also glad that I was able to tell you what sort of person I am. A killer."

*No, never that.*

His grandda come out onto the deck and smiled at them both. He told them that the boys were on their way, and did he want to get dressed. Shep said that he did, and Mr. Marshall let him in the house. Then he sat down beside her.

"I have been thinking on you not calling me anything but Mr." She told him that she was sorry about that. "No worries, but I'm going to start calling you Ms. Parker. That way, I don't have to feel so bad about my manners when I call you Harrison."

"You sly old devil you." He laughed, and asked her if she liked his plan. "Not as much as I do you, Grandda."

"You've made this old man feel like king of the world, my child. Thank you for that." Harris kissed him on his weathered cheek, and then wiped at the tear there. "I miss the women in my life more and more every day, child. Having you here, calling me Grandda, it gives me comfort like you cannot believe. They were my princesses, and I their Prince Charming. My wife told me that I would forever be the one atop her white steed. I love you, Harrison. I surely do."

"I think that I love you too. I don't really know what love is, to be honest with you. My parents had it, a great deal of love for each other. But for me to love again? I'm not sure." He told her that she would someday. "When your guest gets here, Grandda, don't forget, she already knows who I am. All right?"

"Yes, I've been briefed, you might say. This is gonna make my grandsons think I'm something special, don't you think?" She told him that she was sure that they already did. "Maybe, but they sure have a slow way of showing it."

"I'm sure that will change too. They're so busy with their lives, you know. Perhaps it was time that you showed them that you're not an old man without a brain, but a powerhouse of knowledge that they'll never get in time to use."

He was still laughing when he went into the house.

Harris sat there for several moments before she too went inside. There were things about to happen, and she was glad that she was going to have a front row seat to it all. Grandda had a charming way about him that would help her with things. Like this stupid mate thing with Shep. She would get him killed, and Harris wasn't sure that she could live through another family of hers being murdered by jackasses. And to her, most people were just that. Jackasses.

# *Chapter 5*

Lily wasn't the least bit nervous about this. She'd done this twice before for her husband over the years. Today was different in that she would have to be able to entertain a group of people for an hour. She wasn't sure that she could do that. Even though she was in the public eye all the time, she was actually a very shy and quiet person.

The house had been gone over twice before she was to arrive. Getting out of the big limo, she saw the elderly man standing on the front stoop. Mr. Marshall had been her friend and confidant when she'd been a teenager. He'd also been her grandda when she'd needed him to be.

Hugging him, she heard him sob and couldn't help but join him. They both had lost so much when Jill Ann had died. So much more than anyone would ever know of. She was then taken into the house, only to stop and be hugged in a powerful hug once again.

"Oh, Grandda, I'm so sorry for your loss. For you to lose two of the most beautiful people in the world just makes my heart hurt badly." He told her that he'd been ready to join his wife, then found out about Jill Ann. "I don't know if I could have survived any of it, living with them all this time. My goodness, they were both two peas in a pod, weren't they? You'd never know that they weren't related by blood."

"I'm thinking that is what made them so inseparable." Lily agreed with him and went into the large living room that his family was in. My goodness, she thought, they were so big. "Lily, honey, I'd like you to meet my family. You remember some of them when they were — "

"Grandda, you know the first lady? The president's wife?" So he'd not told them who was coming, Lily thought. The sly old bugger would do that to her. Smiling at the men, she shook each of their hands as she was introduced to them. Shep was last, and she looked up into his eyes that were so much like his mother's.

"You look like her. Her eyes, they shine back at me when I see you." Shep thanked her. "She and I — Jill Ann and I — went to school together. All the way from kindergarten through college. Your mother kept me from failing classes. A great many of them, I believe."

"She was as smart as she was beautiful." She looked to his left and saw a young woman there. She was beautiful too, Lily thought. But she had a hardness about her that made her think that she wasn't one to mess with. "I'm sorry, this is my future wife, when I can get her to say yes, Harrison Parker. Harrison, this is First Lady Lily Steele." This was the woman, Lily knew, that she had to get a message to.

Taking her hand was simple. Getting the thumb drive to her hand was that easy too. The sticky tape that was on it would make sure that she didn't drop it or have the need to stick it in her pocket right away, in the event that anyone was looking at them. Even her team of secret service would never know that the two of them had just made a drop, so to speak. Lily so loved all the intrigue.

"Mr. Marshall, I should like to use your office for a moment. I would like to call my husband and tell him that I've arrived safely." Shep told her that he would show it to her. "Thank you so much for this. You have a lovely home. My goodness, is that a herd of deer out there?"

Just as they walked to the doors to the outside deck so that she could get a closer look, she quietly asked him if she could arrange his office. He looked at her oddly, but nodded. Then she asked to be left alone to make the call, and everyone, including the secret service, walked out of the room. She locked the door behind them.

Taking out her cell phone, she called Howard to tell him that she'd arrived just fine, and that everything here was just as lovely as he'd guessed it would be. That was code for everything was going fine so far. Lily promised him, just before hanging up, that she'd make sure to call him when she left. All the men in the room, only men that Howard trusted, were ready to get started.

As soon as she left the office, she went back to the living room. And just as the two men that had waited outside the door were supposed to do, they followed her. Things were going too smoothly, and it made her slightly nervous.

Step one had been to get Harris the thumb drive. Check, she told herself. Step two had been to get the men into the office of the home so that they might make it as secure as possible. She could check that off her list as well. At the other end of the property a building was going up, one that, once completed, would be a situation room for Harris to find out who had betrayed her.

Lily thought she'd make a good spy, except for the part where she had to outrun someone or shoot them. She didn't like the sight of blood. That would, she was sure, make it so that she'd never survive doing what Harris did for her country.

It had never been so easy for her to have fun at gatherings. Not only were the Marshall men all as polite as she'd ever met, but they were unfailingly good to Harris. Especially Shep. The man was completely besotted with his new mate, and that made Lily glad that she'd been able to come here too. To witness the first blossoms of love between two people.

When her cell vibrated in her pocket, it was a signal that the upgrade to the office was finished. They would move out of that room and to the building that she was sure was close to being done, if it wasn't already. Things had a way of getting done quickly when the president was involved.

Looking at her watch, Lily couldn't believe that two hours had gone by. "I have taken up enough of your time." They all said that it had been their pleasure to have been able to talk to her. "Your mother would be so proud of you boys. I know that you're men, but Jill Ann called you that so often that I did wonder if she needed her eyes checked. My goodness, I will miss her."

She would too. Jill Ann had had her private number, and they would try and call at least once a month. To think that it had only been one day before she was killed that they'd last spoken.

Lily stood up. Her job here was finished, but she so hated to leave. "I'll come back here. I promise. It feels so wonderful getting away from Washington to sit with old and new friends. Thank you for this, Sheppard. It has been one of the finest days I've had in a long while." He hugged her again, much to the discomfort of the men with her. "You'll have to come and see me sometime. Howard would love that. We could give you a grand tour of the house, and you can be so impressed with my changes. Not that there have been that many. I'm a woman that likes to get things done that matter, rather than making a room look pretty."

Harris agreed with her, and she wanted to take her into her arms and hug her. The girl was all that stood between the United States and war at times. Yet there was not a soul out in the real world that knew a thing about her. She had even managed to save some people that were less deserving than some, but it was what they gave that was important at the moment they were returned home or, sadly, killed.

Lily went back to the office to make the call to Howard and to unlock the door. If anyone were to enter the room now they'd see nothing out of the ordinary. But she knew better, and so would Harris when she saw it. The thumb drive that had been given to her, Lily knew, would give her the added information that she needed to figure this out. Howard already had an idea who it was that had tried to kill Harris, but he'd not said in his recording. All he said was, he had all the confidence in the world that she'd take care of this threat.

As soon as she was home, Lily met with Howard in his office. She told him how lovely of a time she'd had. Told him about the new mate, as well as how it had felt good to talk to someone that had known Jill Ann as well as she had. Then he held her while she cried, and it felt like the one she'd gotten from Sheppard when she'd left—warm, hopeful, and full of comfort. There would be more conversation in their bedroom when he was finished for the day, and she was looking forward to telling him everything that she'd not been able to say downstairs.

Lily knew that there was no doubt that Harris wouldn't do just as she was told to do. Thankfully, she didn't follow rules very well. Nor did she listen to people that were supposed to be better at things, like kidnapping people. Harris had her own methods, her own ideas about how things should go. Adaptable too when the situation wasn't what she'd been told it was when she went in.

Harris had good people working with her. A great many more that worked under her. She wasn't known to them, not by face or name. Just Cora Banks, who didn't have a record of any kind anywhere in the world. No tax records, no pay stubs, and she didn't have a house worth twice, if not more than the one she was currently living in. Lily wondered if Shep had any idea that his wife to be was a thrice over billionaire, and stood to make so much more on her family's position in the tech world before she was forty.

Sitting at her desk, she could see that she had two messages. One was from Sheppard, the other from her hairdresser. Ignoring one for the other, she had to see what Sheppard had to say about her visit to him.

*You made this old man feel so much better, my dear. I'm so happy that you could have a nice visit with us. Next time you'll need to bring Howard with you and we'll have dinner. Dotty still cooks for the household, so you know what sort of desserts there will be to choose from.*

She laughed at his comment. Lily's downfall was pie of any kind. As she continued, she knew that this was from Harris.

*We're finished with upgrading the things around the property, thank goodness. They surely can make a mess when they wish. I cannot wait to hear from you again.*

The building was completely finished. Lily would have to tell Howard. Also, the mess that they'd left her would be straightened out soon enough. One thing that Harris could do was mess with computers. Having all the equipment that she'd need at the building, the woman could build any kind of supercomputer that she wanted and no one would be the wiser.

Lily's secretary came in just as she was forming the letter back to the man in her head. Shelly hadn't been her first choice in secretaries, but she'd been highly qualified and didn't get on her nerves too much. Telling her about her day tomorrow and the meetings that she had, Lily decided two things.

First, she was going to fire the woman. There wasn't any point in her working with someone that she didn't feel good around. Secondly, and this was most important, she was going to pick her own fucking secretary from now on. That elicited a giggle from her, and Shelly asked her if she was all right.

"Yes, just thinking about my day." She looked up at the women, and decided that there was really something so distrustful about her. Lily didn't know what it was, but something made her feel dirty today, dirtier than she'd felt before. "I would think you'd have some vacation time coming,

Shelly. How long do you have?"

Taken aback, just what Lily had hoped for, she got an honest answer. She'd learned that so long ago, she'd forgotten about it until then. But she knew now that she was going to insist that Shelly take her month of vacation, starting tomorrow. Lily told her that.

"I'm fine, Mrs. Steele. Don't worry about me." The laughter was forced, and Lily didn't care for her tone, either. Instead she told her that she insisted that she go. "I don't mind working through my vacation for you. You're the best boss I've ever had."

"What sort of boss would I be if I let you work like that without any vacation? No, you'll go tomorrow, and that will be the end of it." Lily was glad that she'd been looking at her in the mirror as she fixed her makeup. She might have missed seeing the pure anger on her face when she turned her back on the other woman. "Besides, what sort of mental health advocate would I be if I made my own staff work too hard?"

By the time she'd made the girl get out of her rooms, Lily was exhausted. But she needed to make a phone call, one that had to be done right now. Calling the office of the secret service, she told them that Shelly Main was going on an extended vacation, and that her badge needed to be disabled while she was gone.

It was protocol, she knew that, in the event that her badge was stolen or she left it someplace out in the open. Very few offices did it, but in this, Lily wanted to make sure that things were done right. She did not want the woman coming back into the building until she was ready for her. Then she made a clandestine call to Harris.

"Shelly Main."

Giving her the rest of the information that Lily had on file in her own offices, she hung up her phone and put it back under the jewelry box in her bedroom. Whatever Harris was able to give her was going to be more than she had right now. And that was squat, as far as she was concerned.

~*~

Shep looked over the paperwork that he'd been handed twenty minutes ago. Yes, he'd offered to help, but he didn't have the slightest clue what he was supposed to be looking for. He looked at Harris when she said his name.

"You're not *looking* for anything. I just want you to look at it and see if anything at all jumps out at you." He still didn't get it. "Look. You look at things all the time. Stuff you've looked at a thousand times before, right? Well, I want you to think this is your phone bill and you're looking at it. Just a casual glance. Does anything seem out of the ordinary for a phone bill to you?"

He started to tell her that he was sorry to have offered. There was nothing that he could see, and he was wasting her time. Then he saw it. Just a small glance at the paper that had him seeing the same number over and over. Not only that, it was called at the exact same time every day. He kept staring at the number coming up hundreds of times throughout all eleven sheets of paper.

"The same number. The call is being made every day at the same time." She asked him to show her. "See, one-seventeen in the afternoon. Every day."

"I didn't see the time." That made him feel pretty good. "I did see the numbers, but the rest wasn't there for me. I think I was looking too hard for something else. Thank you."

Shep felt like he'd won everything in the basket. She

71

handed him another stack of papers. This time she had him looking for an address. Harris said that when she'd read it over the first time, she'd forgotten to write it down. That took him two hours to find, as he had hopes that he'd only have to find the number and go from there. But it, like the rest of the wording, was written out.

Stack after stack of sheets of paper were handed to him with something to look for. He would highlight what he found, stack it with the ones he'd finished, then go to the next pile. This went on for several hours before Harris finally stood up to stretch.

She was a beautiful woman, slim and full of energy. Her muscles were tight too. Shep knew that she ran daily. And while he wanted to join her on these early morning excursions, he knew that she did it to be alone, to think. Harris hadn't told him that—he knew from talking to his grandda.

"Shep, your dad is here." Shep stood up and started to ask Harris to stay in here when his grandda came into the room. "The fool thinks that I'm just going to fork over whatever he wants. Well, I'm done with him taking and taking from me."

"Grandda can you stay in here with—?"

"You tell me to hide in this room with your grandda and I will make you eat those words. Between you and I, I think I'm better equipped to handle him than you are." He asked her how. "I have a gun, and I'm not related to the fucker. I know that rule. You can't hurt your sire unless he's causing pain or death to one of your own. You know he doesn't have your brothers, and your grandda is right here. So fuck that shit of hiding behind your large muscles."

"You think I have large muscles?" He had no idea why that caused him to laugh, but he started showing off for her.

When she stalked by him, he grabbed her arm to stay her for a moment. "You don't know him well, but he's slick and he's a fucking bastard. Don't let him in the house if you can help it. Once inside, as sire, he can order me out."

"Oh, he won't come in. Of that, you can be sure." She went out of the room and Shep looked at his grandda, who was smiling.

"Grandda, I'm in love with her." Grandda laughed like he'd told him the best joke ever. "Why is that funny? I love her."

"Of course you do, son. I've known that for some time now. She loves you too, but is a mite afraid of it. Not you, but love. It's not done her any good so far, if I remember her family right." Shep told him that Harris had told him about it. "She would have. Not told too many others I'm betting, either. Well, we should go and see what is going to happen to your daddy. The moron just isn't going to give up."

Shep didn't go all the way into the hall where Harris was talking to his father. She was blocking him with her body, which even though she was slight and shorter than his father, it looked to him like Dad was afraid of her. He might be too, if someone like her was standing in front of him. Harris was a sight, that was for sure.

"You will move, young lady, or so help me, I'll move you."

That was all the threat it took, apparently, for Harris to go from talking to his dad to taking it to the next level. When she brought out her gun and put it to his father's head, he nearly went to her, but thought that she'd just be pissed at him. Besides, she had it under control. Shep did listen better now.

"Listen here, you dumb, moronic, fucking prick. I know what sort of person you are and how you treat people. I am not going to allow you to push people around, especially that sweet man, your father, any longer." Shep glanced at his dad just in time to see him puff out his chest. "You aren't welcome here. In actuality, I don't think you were ever welcome here. This house now belongs to me and Shep. Grandda is living here and under our protection. If you—"

"Protection? Under you? Whatever for? You can't think that— What has he told you? It's all lies. I never once hit him, except when he didn't do as he was told. If he told you that I took money out of his checking account, it's because I was short and he had me driving him around town. Do you have any idea how many times I had to take him out to the fucking cemetery? Jesus, Mary, and Joseph. If I had to spend one more day out there, I was going to kill myself." Harris asked him why he hadn't done that yet. "What? Kill myself? I'd never do that. What are you talking about?"

"I was wrong about you, Mr. Marshall. You're not a moron. You're a fucking idiot." He asked to see his son. Shep moved up behind Harris and looked at his father. He looked bad, he thought, and if the smell was any indication, he hadn't had a shower in some time either. "Well, idiot, he's here. What is it you want? We don't have all day for you. Say it and get away from here."

"What is it, Dad? Before you answer that, I'm not going to give you any money. I don't have a car you can borrow, nor do I have a single place you can stay." Dad actually glared at him. "It might do you well to remember that I'm not a child any longer, you have a gun at your forehead, and she's going to kill your ass if you don't fucking straighten up and do what she tells you."

"You letting pussy run your life now, son? Not a way to go. I got myself sucked into that once with your momma. Didn't— Mother fuck, what the hell are you doing? Are you trying to kill me?" Harris had fired a shot to the left of his father's head. It had to hurt his hearing, but all Shep could do was laugh.

"Had I wanted you dead, idiot, you'd be dead. I don't miss." He believed her. And so did his dad, because he took a step back and looked at him. "Don't look to him for help, mister. If he knew half the things about you that I do, he would have been justified in killing you a long time ago."

"Like what?" His dad looked around, either for help that wasn't going to be coming or calculating the distance between him and the road. "What did you do, Dad? Who did you hurt that I'm going to have to kill you for?"

"I didn't do anything. She's...she's full of shit." Dad backed away more. He had nearly tripped over his feet twice trying to get off the porch and onto the drive. "I'll just come back when you're less busy entertaining. I can see that you're very busy now. I'll just...later."

They both watched him as he ran toward the road like the hounds of hell were after him. Just as Shep was going to step out onto the porch too, just to see which direction he'd gone, Grandda started laughing so hard that he thought for sure that he was going to hurt himself.

"Oh crap, did you see that? He ran like he was going to have someone shooting at him. Holy crap, he sure was scared of you, Harrison, honey." He was still laughing when she shut the door. "Shep, did you see that? I bet he'd have wet his pants if she'd pushed him a little more. Darn it, I surely wish

75

that I had a camera about now. I would have— My phone. I had it with me right here. I could have.... Oh well. Next time I'll get him on camera. He's going to be coming back, you know."

Shep looked at both of them, his grandda and Harris. They knew something, and he wanted to know what it was. But before he could ask, Harris cut him off. She did that a lot, he thought.

"Don't be getting your underwear all twisted up. I took care of it. Why do you think he's coming here now?" He asked what it was she'd done to him, and why. "He was harassing one of the women in town. By harassing, I mean he was trying to get her to suck him off in the form of payment for his meal. She was kinda shook up about it, and I saw her a few minutes later at the bank. By the way, you have to go there sometime today and sign some shit. But about your father, I didn't touch him. Not yet, at any rate, but he won't be bothering any women in the future. Not around here, anyway. They all think he has fleas."

"How did they come to that conclusion?" Harris said that she'd taken out an ad in the paper and announced it. "That's slander—you know that, don't you? He could sue you and more than likely win."

"No, it would have to be untrue if that were the case." Grandda pointed out that he was a cat, a jaguar. That he couldn't have those. "Well, he is an animal, and he has been sleeping in the wild. And he believes it enough to not say a word when I told him about it. He does, however, have lice. Badly, as a matter of fact. Maybe that's what he has and he thinks it's the other. Gonorrhea is a nasty thing, I've heard. Either way, I'd not let him borrow a comb or brush if I were you."

"What about the bank?" Her face heated up. "You brought it up. I'm just wondering what it is the bank wants of me."

"I was in there when my attorney called me to talk. The only other person in the world that knows anything about me and my inheritance is Ricky West, my attorney. You need to go there and sign some paperwork to put your name on things with mine. That way if I'm killed, it won't go to the state or some other stupid shit." Shep wasn't sure if she was serious or not, but he told her that he didn't want her to get killed, not at all. But said he'd go in today, then asked if she would go with him. "Sure. I have some stuff to get anyway. I think your grandda needed to run some errands too."

Shep asked his grandda what was going on when Harris went into the office to work. Grandda didn't look like he wanted to answer, but when he did, Shep wasn't sure that he was telling him the truth.

"She's worth a good deal more than we are. Even adding us all together. I'm guessing that she wants you to have it should she die, just like she said." He asked who was going to kill her. "You were here when Lily was here. What sort of person do you think can have the president's wife come around to hand off stuff? And what sort of people would like her not to be around anymore? Pretty powerful, I'd say. Wouldn't you?"

"Yes."

He waited until Grandda went down the hall before he looked at the office door. There was more to this than he was seeing. Perhaps he needed to think on it for a while, or just wait to see what the bank had to say. Whatever it was, he had a feeling that he was in for a bigger shock than his father had been.

# Chapter 6

There were only two people that could have ordered her death. One of them she thought was dead, the other she had assumed was a friend of the president. Either way, she'd not ever looked into their lives until today. The phone calls were something that she had yet to figure out as well.

Why call at the same time, every day? Who was at the other end only answering the phone, then both parties hanging up? Was it saying something? A clue of some sort? She wanted to figure it out so badly that she hurt with it.

Then she had an idea. Call the number that was putting the calls out and pretend to be something like a survey taker, and then hold them on the line until it was well past the time for the call to be made. Harris wondered how that would help. And if the other person were to say something, would she know the voice? It was worth a shot, and one that she was going to have to put off until tomorrow. She'd missed her opportunity for the day, as it was after the time. She wasn't sure yet if this was the best plan, anyway. Harris was just tossing out ideas.

"Are you ready, love?" She looked at Shep when he called out to her. "What's the matter? Have you found something you can use?"

"No. Not...why do you care what happens to me? There has to be a reason, right? I mean, if I were to be killed or something, wouldn't you be a free and clear of having a mate?" Shep came into the room with her and closed the door behind him. "If you're going to yell at me or something, I want to remind you that I have a gun."

"I'm not going to yell at you. Also, I'm well aware that you're armed all the time. It's what keeps me from pulling your body flush with mine and having my way with you." She let out a long breath when he was standing in front of the desk she'd taken over. "Harrison, you've been driving me insane since you arrived and I figured out what you are to me. I want nothing more than to take you beneath me, or even against the wall, and pound you until both of us are too exhausted to move again."

"There are things about me that you aren't aware of. Or perhaps you are. I don't know. But they're not good things." He nodded as if he knew everything. "Do you know? Or are you saying that to get laid?"

"I know very little about you other than what you have shared with me. I could have, I suppose, looked you up, but that seemed like snooping around, and that bothered me as well. Come here, Harrison, I would love to kiss you." She stood up twice before sitting back down. "Are you afraid of me?"

"No, I'm not. Not afraid of you, but of how you're going to make me feel. I'm afraid of loving you too, if you want

the truth. I'm afraid that you're going to leave me as well."
He told her that he wouldn't. Not ever. "You say that, but
you might get sick to death of me. And if you point out that
you're a shifter and that they love for life, remember, I've had
dealings with your father. He is far from loveable."

"Come here, love." She wanted to tell him no, wanted
to say that she liked it just where she was. But her feet were
moving around the desk before she could convince herself
this was a terrible idea. More than that, it was the worst of all
ideas, going to him. "I will never harm you. With words or my
hands. I won't leave you, because without you, I don't think
that I could live another moment. I do love you. I've tried
hard not to tell you since I figured it out today. I know that I
have to take my time, woo you some. You're very skittish for
someone as tough as you are."

"I've been hurt. Not by men. I don't allow them to get
close enough to— Are you going to kiss me or not?"

Shep seemed to have been waiting for that signal. For her
to ask him to touch her. Because when he kissed her, devoured
her completely, she knew that for the rest of her life, no one
would ever be able to mark her like this kiss was doing to her.

He didn't touch her anywhere else but her face. It wasn't
enough for her. Her body seemed to be demanding more of
him than Harris thought that she could take. When Shep lifted
his head, he had to hold her steady because she felt as if she
were ready to fall down. Looking up at him, she thought for
sure there would be a smirk. At the very least, a look that told
her that he'd known it would be her begging for this.

Instead, he looked thoughtful, like he was trying to
decide if he had enjoyed the kiss or not. Backing away from
him, she didn't struggle when he pulled her back, his arms

around her tightly, and kissed her again, and this time there was no doubt that both of them were enjoying the kiss. It was everything that she'd ever imagined it would be to have a man that loved her kiss her.

Shep touched her back, her ass and arms. Her face and neck felt the touch of his fingers. Harris moaned against his mouth when he lifted her higher so that her body lined up with his, and they were breast to chest, groin to pussy.

This time when he lifted his head, she saw the power and the raw emotion there. It was the sexiest and the most beautiful thing she'd ever seen. Touching her fingers to his cheek, she could feel the stubble of his beard as he leaned into her hand, as well as the strong line of his chin and, most importantly, the pounding of his pulse at his throat.

"If my grandda wasn't waiting in the car for us, I'd say bedamned with going to town and take you right here on the floor. Or the wall. Anywhere that I thought sturdy enough to withstand my pounding you." Harris felt her legs tremble when he set her down on the floor. She wouldn't let him hold her; it was as if his touch were just too much. "Steady now. If you fall, I'm not going to be responsible for not jumping you."

"I'm all right. No, that's not true. I don't think I'll ever be all right again." Shep laughed a little. "I feel like I've been kissed by an electrical wire. I can honestly say that I've never felt like that after a kiss."

"Me either." She looked at him to see if he was joking. "I'm serious. I've kissed women before, but that—that was unlike anything I've experienced, ever. I don't think that I will with any other person again."

Jealousy rolled over her, like she were being drenched in it. Instead of opening her mouth and saying something really possessive and stupid, she said she was going to the car. But Shep stopped her before she got much further than a couple of steps.

"I won't." She tried to jerk away from him. "Harrison, I won't ever touch another woman for as long as I live. I didn't mean for it to come out that way." She wanted to deny that she'd felt anything from his hurtful words, but it would have been a lie and she didn't want to lie to him. "I'm so sorry I said that. I am."

"I've never been jealous before." He nodded, not laughing at her or even smiling. "It was like I wanted to murder every woman in the world in those seconds. I didn't want to say something stupid either. So I was going to go."

"Don't turn from me when I hurt you. I might not have thought of how my words sounded to you had I not seen the look on your face. You're the first woman that I've ever loved for my own. I know that I can be a crude bastard. I spent a great deal of time around men and women who didn't take into account others' feelings. Nor what a misplaced word could do to someone. I am truly sorry." Nodding, she leaned into his chest. It was large and warm. Also as hard as a stone. "I love you, Harrison. But if we don't move soon and take Grandda to town, I'm afraid that he'll drive himself."

They were walking to the car when she reached for his hand. It was much larger than hers, by a great deal, but he held it like it was made of porcelain, and she loved that feeling. In fact, she thought that she could get used to holding hands with him.

The ride in was made with Grandda doing most of the talking, about the things that he had to take care of and picking up his mail. It was a surprise to her to realize that no mail came out to the farm. Something about it being the only one on the road for several hundred miles. Whatever the reason, she thought that he enjoyed going to the post office. It was somewhat of a social time for him.

Leaving him at the office, she and Shep went to the bank. Shep's cell was ringing even before they got to see the bank manager, and he stepped outside to talk while she went to the man's desk. His name eluded her, so she was glad for his name being displayed on his desk. Mr. Ronald Ballinger.

"I've done all that you asked, Ms. Parker. I had no idea there were so many assets that hadn't been taken care of for you." She told him that she'd been too busy to keep up with it. "I've also spoken to your attorney. Mr. West. He's of the opinion that you'll be keeping your home. I told him that we'd not discussed it."

"I don't know what to do with it." He nodded, but said little more about it as Shep joined them finally. "Mr. Ballinger was asking me about my house. I told him that I don't know what to do about it."

"Where is it?" She told him it was only about a mile from there. "Really? I guess I had no idea that you had lived so close to us. Do you want to sell it or keep it? I'm easy about that. Grandda thinks that it's a fairly large estate that you have."

"It is—large, I mean. The house is huge too." She didn't want to tell him that she'd come from a long line of monied people, but the banker had no such trouble. "Yes, I told you that I had an inheritance. I've not done anything with it since I was old enough to take the running of the companies over. The house was in my dad's family for a very long time. I mean, it's since been updated, several times. But not since they were killed."

Mr. Ballinger handed a file full of papers that Shep would need to sign. He just looked at her and asked if she was sure about this. She nodded once, and he started signing his name where the tabs were. When he was done, Harris wondered if he realized that he'd be a billionaire. Or even if he'd care.

It took him ten minutes to sign all the papers. Not once did he ask what it was for, nor did he ask her if she was sure again. Harris did wonder if he did that often—signed his name to things that he never read. But as soon as he handed the papers back to Mr. Ballinger, he assured her, without her asking, that he'd never done that before. Harris felt better then.

"All right. I'm to ask you several things before we continue. The house, which we have talked about. Mr. West was wondering what your plans were for it." She looked at Shep when Ballinger continued on about it. "You could both go and have a look at it. After all this time, it might be something that you wish to keep. Or you could decide if you want to sell it off or not."

"You have no opinion on this?" Mr. Ballinger asked Shep what he meant. "I don't know. I guess I thought you knew something about the house, and could tell us if it was a good time to sell or not. Or something like, it would be a shame to sell something so old."

He laughed. "When I spoke to Mr. West, he assured me that the best way to get you to do something was to tell you that you couldn't. He said that most of the time it worked, but there have been times when Ms. Parker here has bitten his head off. I think he meant seriously. I wish to keep my head where it belongs." Ballinger laughed again. "To be honest, I know nothing about the house, nor did I know much about the young lady here. I can say that I don't know that much more, but I am sorry for what you went through, miss. I am terribly sorry for your loss as well."

"Thank you." She didn't want anyone to talk about her parents. Not a stranger anyway. "If everything you needed is taken care of, perhaps we can go out and see the house and make a decision then. We'll be back sometime tomorrow, all right?"

"Yes, all right. I do have more questions regarding the estate, but we can get to that when you've made a decision." She nodded and hurried out of the bank. Shep held her when she stopped suddenly by the car. Breathing hard, she focused on his voice as he kept talking to her about the weather, until she finally felt like she could stand on her own.

"You all right now?" She nodded. "I'm guessing that you're not good with people giving you condolences, are you?"

"No, not really. It makes me remember things all over again." He asked her if she'd be all right going through the house. "I think, with you there, I will be able to. All the clothing that belonged to my parents and myself has been removed. All of my toys donated to some charity. The books are there, along with furniture that would be outdated. The house has been cleaned every season change, everything covered up, but I've not been in there since that night."

"Did you want to go now?" She told him that she thought that she did. "All right then. Let me get Grandda, then we'll head over there. He might have some insight on the selling or keeping it market that few know. I've only come to realize that Grandda is pretty smart and full of knowledge."

That made her feel good, that he'd taken her advice and

made the elderly Marshall feel good about himself. Getting into the car when he came back with his grandda, she thought about the house. She was both looking forward to seeing it and did not want to see it. Only time would tell.

~*~

Shep didn't know what he had expected in the house. Certainly nothing like this. It was a house straight out of a romance novel, he was sure of that. The grounds alone made him not envy the person who had to take care of it. There were flowers and trees all over the gentle slope leading up to the big mansion.

The drive curved around in front of the three-story home, which was made of dark brown brick. The shutters were painted a dark blue that went well with the urns on the front porch. The flowers there were of the same hue, and he wondered if they were grown on this property so that they might be assured of matching the house.

The brick stairs that led up to the house were so wide that he could have parked his new SUV along the front of it six or seven times, bumper to bumper, and had plenty of room left over. But at the top, where it met with the front doors, it was only about two cars wide. The people standing there looked like they had stepped out of the 1800s to meet with the lord and lady of the house. The butler coming toward them greeted them all three, and he was happy to know that they'd been not only expected, but the house had been readied for them.

"Mr. Marshall, I'm glad to finally meet you, sir. My name is Taylor. The household is ready to meet you as well." He looked at Harris. "Ms. Harrison, it's been a very long time, indeed. I must say that you look so much like your mother that I didn't know what to say to you."

"Thank you, Taylor. I've been sending funds to update the house. Have you been able to get anything done?" He assured her that all was well. "Good. I've come here to make a decision with Mr. Shep. I don't know what my plans are for the house."

If the butler was upset about it, he didn't even blink to show it. After introducing him and his father to the staff, and telling Harris who was new or not, Taylor led them into the main hall. And good Christ, what an entrance hall it was.

Shep looked at the artwork on the walls, the large paintings that were as old as his grandda was, or older. He walked to the first one, with a frame that looked like it had been dipped in gold. He could see the signature in the corner and turned to look at Harris.

"Yes, it's who you think it is." He pointed to it again. "Yes, Shep, I know. My grandfather was good friend with the artist, and bought it from him to help him out. I think it's worth a great deal more than he paid him back then."

The rest of the house was just as well appointed. The dining room was something that he wanted badly. It was long and had a table in the room that would seat as many as fifty guests, he'd bet. The chairs were lined up along both sides of it like soldiers, with one at each end to keep the company in line. The chandelier was magnificent, and so bright that he was sure once the lights were turned on there wouldn't be a darkened corner in the entire room.

The study was just as beautiful. Books were on each shelf, with their titles showing in the dim light. Several conversation areas, as he thought they were called, were all around too. A large fireplace sat in one corner, dark now that it was warm outside, but he could see it lit up in the winter with candles and pictures over the wide imposing mantel.

There was no overhead lighting in this room, but he could see the tin ceiling. It was darkening with age, and he was happy to see that no one had painted over it. Sitting in one of the chairs when Harris had to take a call, Tayler asked him if they were to be wed.

"When I can get her to tell me she will. I've asked her a couple of times, but I think I'm wearing her down." He nodded. Shep wondered if he had a sense of humor. "What do you think of her selling the home? I think she's been afraid of the memories that surround this place."

"I'm sure that she has. We have replaced every piece that those men dared to touch. The dining room table and the chairs too. The master bedroom has no furniture as yet, but all the carpets were taken up and the floor sanded to its original wood. It's very lovely there. Also, all the paintings were insured, so they have been replaced with something similar. The house is quite old, sir. It has been in Ms. Harrison's family for a number of generations." Shep told him that Harris had mentioned that. "I worry for her, if I may say. She has endured so much over her short lifetime."

"She has. I'm going to make it my life's work to make sure that she has a better time in life from now on. I love her very much."

Taylor might have been about to say something, but Harris came into the room then. She looked upset.

"Everything all right, Harris?" He took her hand into his and she looked at him. "What is it? Tell me what it is so I can slay the dragon for you."

Taylor left them then and he told her he was sorry. "I don't think he was upset, just leaving us alone for a few minutes." She looked around. "This room was my father's favorite place to be. He spent a great deal of time in here going over the books that he needed information from, and writing his own. The call was from my contact in the Department of Homeland Security. Shelly Main isn't a person. I believe it's a fake name, though I can't be sure. I'm following something that has her related to the VP. I'm thinking that's what it is, so that no one will connect her to him. I now have to figure out who she is, and then tell Lily. Whoever she is, she's going to have a great number of questions to answer. Especially if she's Benson's daughter."

"Is Lily in trouble? I mean, is she safe?" Harris told him how Shelly was on vacation, one that Lily had made her take. And that Lily had also disabled her badge. "I'd go a little further than that, if I were her. I'd circulate her picture so that everyone is aware of who she might be."

"I've done that through the secret service." Harris thanked him for thinking of that. "I need to get my mind off of this for a little while. Are you ready to see the rest of the house? It's not nearly as bad as I thought it would be coming back here."

"Grandda is in the kitchen. He said he could smell something baking. I swear, Harris, that man has a nose for baked goods like no one I've ever met before." He opened the door and found that two of the staff were there with the butler. Taylor turned to him and asked if he could answer a question please. "Sure. I mean, I can try, but I'm new to this household."

"Your grandda said that you're not selling, and that you'll be having dinner here this evening. I thought that I would ask if he was prone to making plans without making sure."

Shep said that his grandda was prone to a lot of things that he shouldn't be doing. "Would you like to stay to dinner? I'm afraid that we're not prepared as we'd be if we'd had more notice, but I think we can make a nice meal for the three of you."

"Do you have enough for eight, Taylor?" He told Harris that he could feed an army should she give him an hour. "Yes, well, you might think you're feeding one after you meet the rest of Shep's family. If they can make it, I'll make sure to let you know. Something else that you might already be aware of, Shep and his family are cats—jaguars. Will that be a problem?"

"No, my lady. I don't foresee it being anything like that. He will know too that there are others in the household that aren't human." Harris told the elderly man that she'd figured that out. "If you're all right with showing the house to Mr. Sheppard on your own, I'll have a conversation with cook now, and we'll await hearing from you about the others. All right?"

There were eight bedrooms in the house, most of which had been closed off. The furniture in the rooms was covered up with large sheets, but he could tell that the rooms had been swept recently. He noticed that they had skipped one of the bedrooms, and he could only assume it had been hers. The master suite was right in front of her when she turned and looked at him.

"This room is empty of most all of the things that were in here that night. Nothing was saved from it. Even the things that were undamaged were tossed out. I told Taylor when I was able to take over things for myself that I wanted nothing in here to remind me of that night." He told her that he understood. "The room at the other end of the hall was mine. I've avoided it, but I think that if I can go into the master, with you, that I'll be able to go into that room as well. I'm sorry that I'm so unsure of myself right now."

"Honey, there are fresh memories in here even if they are very old ones. I've heard from my brothers, and they're coming to dinner. They're excited to see the house. I only told them that we're undecided about it for now. Are you still?" She didn't know, Harris told him. "I can understand that too. But I will tell you, this is the most beautiful house that I've ever had the pleasure of going through."

"Will you be all right here if I decide to keep it? And your grandda, will he stay with us? I've grown very fond of the old man." Shep said that so long as there were baked goods around, his grandda would stay in a barn. "I don't think we'd have to go that far, but there is one of those too. Also, there are a great many other things here that I couldn't stand to part with. We'll look those over too."

As soon as she threw open the two doors that led into the master bedroom, Shep knew that he'd beg her to stay here. It was a room that someone could sleep soundly in and enjoy the outdoors too. From the hardwood floors to the large wrap around porch that went from one of the large glass doors to the other, it was a place that he could see them living in until they pushed up daisies.

The bathroom was bigger than his bedroom at his mom's house. There was not only a tub, but a shower for two, double sinks, and a commode that was behind another huge, closed-off area. Walk in closets were at the other end of the room, along with a vanity for a woman. He moved out of that area out onto the deck, and stood there in awe that this could be his home if she wanted.

"There are over six thousand acres here. Not all of it you can see from here. It's been cut off in a couple of places to make room for the roads that travel to the orchard and the gardens." He asked her what they grew here. "Mainly we only grew what we would eat. The rest was donated to the pantries and such. The orchard is the same way. The cook will bring in extra staff, and they put up the fruit when it is ready and make other things that are put in the large freezers in the sub levels of the house. The water is supplied through an underground water system that was here all along. There are also solar panels on the roof and up on the mountain there that supply the house with electricity. My father did most of the improvements on the house."

"That's wonderful."

They made their way back into the room, and she picked up a phone that he'd not noticed before. She told Taylor that they'd be having eight for dinner, then asked if it would be all right. Apparently he said yes, so she nodded at him.

"I hope that if we decide to keep the house, he doesn't run for the hills after feeding us all."

The bedroom that they'd skipped was next. Harris didn't hesitate at all, but opened the doors to the little girl's room. Her books were still on the shelves. The bed, a bright pink, was made up, and the little pink hearts that were on the spread were in the curtains too. Harris picked up one of the books and handed it to him. It was *Moby Dick*.

Opening the book, he wasn't the least bit surprised to see that it was a signed copy. It was addressed to a man by the name of Hopewell Harrison. He looked at her.

"This was in my mom's family for a great many

generations. But when my grandparents died before having any other children but my mom, she inherited it all. It's called Harrison House. My first name is my mother's maiden name. For a while it was called Parker House, but my dad thought it sounded like they made rolls here, so we just called it Harrison House. If you'd like to live here with me, I'd call it Marshall House, with you."

"I'd very much like to live here with you. Raise children and have my family here. But I'd very much like for you to marry me, Harris. Marry me here in this house, so that your parents can be a part of our day." She nodded. "Thank goodness. I was sure that Taylor would have tossed me to the street if we weren't married soon."

"I have a favor to ask, please?" Shep told her anything. "I'd very much like to combine my rings, if you don't mind. Something of my mom's, her engagement ring, and whatever other piece that you have of your mom's. If you wouldn't mind."

"I think that is an excellent idea, future Mrs. Harrison Parker Marshall. I also think that calling this Marshall House, if you don't mind, would make me very happy." She nodded, and he kissed her. "If we had a bed up here, I'd break it in right now. But, I can hear my family coming anyway, so we'll postpone this for a little while longer."

"I cannot wait."

She left him there with his tongue hanging out, he was sure. Shep was going to have to keep on his toes if he wanted to keep up with her. She was his future wife. He could not wait to tell the rest of them. And the household.

# Chapter 7

Dean wanted the house that Mom had lived in. They decided to maintain his house; it was smaller than the rest of them. So in the event that someone needed a place to lay over they could stay there instead of in a hotel. The swap out was fine with the rest of his brothers, so he took it. As they moved things that Shep wanted to take with him to the new house, people that Harris had hired were all over Marshall House, getting it ready with whatever she needed.

Grandda was beside himself with excitement to be living in a house so prim and proper, and it was a little closer to where Mom and Grandma were both buried. Dean walked around the rooms in his new home, and smiled whenever he saw something that would tug at a memory. He thought about dinner last night in the mansion that Shep and Harris would now be living in.

The brothers had been so nervous about having dinner in the house as soon as they'd gotten out of their cars. Rodney thought they for sure had the wrong house, but when Shep came out to show them around, all of them doubled their fear of fucking up things for their older brother.

Dinner was more than he could have hoped for. Not only were there steaks and baked potatoes as big as his hand, there were other things that made it seem more like he was at a restaurant than having dinner at home.

Garlic twist knots that everyone loved but were afraid to eat more than one of. Bacon cut up into perfect little squares that went with the potatoes. Nothing was served in pans, either. There was no foil around the spud. The butter was in small pats, with a large M in the middle of each one. Green beans that hadn't been broken up were laid like logs on a platter. There were button mushrooms that had some kind of stuffing in them. Dean was actually afraid of some of the dishes. He didn't know what they were, and was afraid of making himself want to spit things out. So he just sat there, with his beautifully done steak and potato, and tried to figure out what to do with his hands. That was until the roll hit him in the forehead. He looked at Harris when she laughed.

"This is going to be our home, guys. What is the matter with you all?" Some mumbled, others said nothing at all. The butler asked what he'd like to drink. "Bring them some beer, Taylor. Maybe it will loosen them up a little. Oh, and will you tell Grace that the rolls are perfect?"

After he left them to get the beers, Dean had stared hard at Harris. There was something about her that he'd not noticed until that moment. She was comfortable in this house. Harris had been born to be rich. She was too, according to Shep. Richer than all of them together.

"Why are we here? For you to show off?" He didn't know why he'd said that, but he had and he wasn't taking it back.

"I mean, this is a house that people wait all their lives for. The meal here is something out of Plate and Platter, if there is such a thing. So why did you invite us here when you had to know this was too much for us?"

Shep stood up, and Dean did as well. Harris told them both to sit down, and while he had a hard time doing what she told him, he finally did. He knew then that he'd hurt her feelings.

"When I was a child, my entire life was shattered in this room. My parents were both killed, and I was a child that had no one left but an aunt that no more wanted me than I did her. But I survived." She looked around the room. "I thought that by inviting you guys here, you could help me make my first good memory in this room. As a family."

He started to tell her that he was sorry, but she cut him off as she stood up. If she left them there, he would be as good as dead, and Dean knew that he would deserve it. But she turned and looked at them all before she spoke again.

"You mother fucker." He felt his eyes widen when she looked at him. "You stupid mother fucker. I swear to Christ, if your mom were here right now…. Well, I'm sure that she'd be as appalled at you as I am."

"I'm so sorry. I don't know why I said that." She told him that wasn't good enough. "Okay, it's not. But I'm uncomfortable, and I don't want to fuck up."

"So you insult me? Well, thank you so much. Are you more comfortable now with yourself? Do you think that if I were to pass you some of the corn pudding, you'd turn your nose up at it?" Dean said he didn't know what the dishes were, so he'd not even be able to pass it to her. "My staff worked very hard on this, because they wanted to impress you as well. The corn pudding is the yellow corn bread looking stuff."

"I'm so sorry. I was embarrassed about how I was feeling, and took it out on you." She glared harder at him. "If it'll make you feel any better, I'll try everything on this table. So long as you tell me what I'm eating."

"There is no poison in any of this, but I might put some in your dessert." He said it was no less than he deserved. "The corn pudding, I've pointed out. There is green bean casserole that is really good, and not at all like you might see on the television with mushroom soup in it."

As he began trying the dishes on the table, all of which he simply loved, she told them what the dishes were. The stuffed mushrooms had a sausage mixture in them that he thought he could have eaten the entire plate full of. There were poached pears that, while the name sounded pretentious, it was one of the best things he'd ever tasted that had pears in it. The bacon, she told him, was from the estate. As were most of the things on the table, including the steaks.

"You're self-reliant here." She nodded at him as he passed her the last of the corn pudding. "I studied that in college. It was more like a fantasy than a reality, I thought. But you've made it work. I'd like to study the land, if you'd not bury me on it anytime too soon."

After that, things were better for him and the rest of the people at the table. Even Heath, who was the shyest of any of them, broke out of his shell and began to tell them what he liked about each thing that he ate. Even after the night he'd spent in his new home, Dean still could taste some of the dishes, and wished he'd not made such a fool of himself. Now he might not ever be invited back, he thought.

He thought of the conversation about the way things

worked there over and over, and wondered if he could ever make it work here. He remembered what she'd told him about her father. Dean had been invited to stay as long as he wanted with each of the foremen to learn whatever he wanted. The dinner, he knew, and the way it had started out would be with him for the rest of his life. In addition to what she had said to him after the dinner was finished.

"I don't have a problem with that, but I can understand why you were feeling that way. Next time, just say something. I'm not going to shoot you unless you call me a snob again." He hadn't, but didn't think this was a good time to point out that he'd not done that. Instead, he had himself another garlic knot with the creamy butter that had been churned there too. "We have about six hundred people that work here at any given time. In the summer months and during the fall harvest, there are more. My dad was proud of the way the land gave him back as much as he tried to give it."

Dean only had a few things that he had to replace in the house. He loved the big television that Shep had used here. As well as the tea maker. Making himself a list of things that he'd need, Dean figured that he'd pick those up after he was finished at the courthouse.

Shep had given up his part of the land. The land that their mother had left them would be divided again, this time only five ways. And his brother Trenton was going to take his part so that he could finish the house that he'd started. Really, all he'd had done was the excavation of the land to put the house in, so it was like Trenton was starting fresh. He was too, Dean thought.

He'd lived in the house that had belonged to their mother last. He'd been there when she got sick one winter and they

99

all thought that she might not make it. But she did, pulling through and getting a little of her old pep back, they thought.

Mom had a garden every year. She grew most of the vegetables that they ate, and canned or froze the rest. They'd never had time to raise beef or pork. They'd all gone to college locally, and she didn't want to take up their studying time, making them do more work than was necessary, so that their grades didn't fail.

Walking to the garage that held his car now, he thought about the car that Mom had been driving the night that she'd been killed. It hadn't been in the best of shape — all of them would agree to that — but it hadn't been unsafe. The tires were almost new, and the engine, once it was going, would run all day without any more trouble. He moved around to the back of the garage to have a look at the wreckage.

The towing company had brought it to the house after they'd pulled it from the ditch. He wasn't sure what they expected them to do with it. The insurance company had totaled it, so there wasn't any value in it. Not to mention, the entire driver's side had been sliced open to get their mother out.

Looking it over, he pulled out his cell phone and asked the towing company if they knew of any scrap places around town. He was given the name of three places, and he got someone to answer on the second ring.

After talking to the man for fifteen minutes, Dean had a list of things that they'd buy from him for cash. Of course, if he brought it to them he'd make more, but at this point, he just wanted the car gone. But as he began looking around, he could see things that had been just lying around, not just collecting dust, but with tall grass around it where they couldn't move it to mow.

After going to the bank and the courthouse, Dean had a list of things that his brothers had that they wished to get rid of too. As he was pulling into his drive, he saw more things. Christ, he could make a killing on just this stuff. Instead, he made a call to the local Boy Scout troop, at Harris's suggestion, and donated all the things they could pile onto the truck for the company coming to get the car, and they could have the cash.

It took him six hours to gather all the things that were being scrapped. He had a truck, but it certainly made it much nicer to gather it with the extra hands of the kids. At dinner time, he was ready to call it a day when Harris and Shep showed up with pizzas and drinks for the kids. Mr. Bishop was taking the last load away when he handed the troop leader a check.

"I had to pick up some things around town too. I was telling the households what I was doing out here, and they donated their things too. Mr. Carol said that you guys should do this once a year, and he'd surely chip in the things that are left at his lot." Mr. Carol ran the mechanics shop in town. "You boys, I think you made short work of things out here for me, so I put in some for you too."

The check was for seven hundred dollars. They were so excited about it that he said that he'd match it. Of course, not to be outdone, Shep said he would as well. The troop really needed new uniforms, as well as their camping trip was coming up and they didn't have all the nicer equipment that they needed. Trenton and Heath said they'd do that for them, and Oakley and Rodney donated the money to get their van fixed. All in all, it was a great day for everyone.

After he mowed in the areas that were in dire need of it, he made sure that he had all the equipment to make his own compost area. His mom had a pile out back that she'd added scraps of food to and such, but he didn't remember her ever using it. Harris helped him put it together and by nightfall, not only did he have his patch of ground ready for late crops, but his compost generator was up and running too. He couldn't believe how much fun he'd had by working his ass off.

Tomorrow he was going to spend the day with one of Harris's workers. He was looking forward to it. Laying out his clothing with the notebook and pens that he wanted to make sure he didn't forget, Dean went to bed. Yes, he thought, he was going to make this farm work, even if it was just for him.

~*~

Shep loved the new bedroom set that they'd ordered before they'd fully moved in. They'd had to get not just a bed for the room, but a chest of drawers and other items that had been removed from the room the night of the murder. The crew that Harris had hired was turning the office that she was going to use into a safe zone for her, and she had several men working for her that would be around the place all the time. Armed men that would shoot before asking questions.

Shep put the bed together and made it before going downstairs to the kitchen. Harris said that she had about two hours of work to do before she would be his for the rest of the day. He hoped so—one more night without having her was going to kill him.

He supposed that he could have taken her anywhere, but that just seemed like a foolish thing to do. They were going to get married on Friday afternoon, and Grandda was giving her away. Not a big ceremony, but it would be held at the house. Shep didn't care so long as she was his forever.

"Sir?" He turned to look at Taylor. "There is a man here to see you. He said that he's your father. I see the resemblance, but he is the most rude man I've met. Demanding that I fetch you like you were nothing more than a dog. He believes that you are working here for the young miss. What a thing to say about you."

"I'll see to him. In the future, you can slam the door in his face and tell him to go away, or call the cops. He's not a nice man at all." Taylor said that he'd remember that. "Do me a favor, will you, Taylor? Invite him in and have him sit in the parlor for me. But don't leave him. He would steal the pennies off a dead man if he could."

"Oh, yes, I can see this. Shall I bring in tea and scones too, sir? Just to show him that you're much better than he is?" He and Taylor laughed, and it felt like they were making progress in becoming friends rather than lord of the house and butler. "I don't normally condone showing off, sir, I want you to know that. But this man is a horror, if you ask me. I'm sorry. I know that he is your father, but—"

"Don't be sorry, Taylor. He's been like that my entire life. Used to knock us around until we got old enough that we frightened him. Mom too, but she started carrying around a ball bat and busted him up a few times before he got the sense to leave her alone too." Taylor huffed and said that wasn't right, and that he'd do what Shep wanted. "Thank you very much. Before you leave, can you tell me where the Parkers had their bed? I don't think I'd want it in the same place, for Harris."

"You have picked a good spot, sir. It's very nice indeed."

103

Thanking him, Shep finished up the bedroom before going downstairs. Meeting his father in the parlor, he was glad to see that Taylor hadn't left him at all. As soon as he entered the room, Taylor said that he'd get them tea.

"That man watched me like I was going to steal something. What did you tell him? Do you think you can get me hired on here with you? I sure could use some cash, boy. Do you happen to have any on you?" He told him no. "No what? I asked you a bunch of things."

"No to all of them. And I don't work here, Dad, I live here."

Dad stared at him for several seconds before bursting out laughing.

When the tea trolley was brought in, Harris followed, saying that she'd pour. Before sitting down, she kissed Shep on the mouth.

"Dad, you remember Harrison, I'm sure. She and I are getting married Friday."

"What sort of fool do you take me for?" Harris said that she could list them, but Dad cut her off. "I wasn't talking to you, bitch, I was talking to my son."

Harris got up and slapped his father so hard that he was knocked back on the seat. Then she sat down again, asking James if he wanted tea or not. He asked why she'd hit him.

"You don't know me well enough to call me bitch. But if you do it again, bitch or not, I'll tear your fucking head off. Now, do you want tea or not? The sooner that you get whatever it is you came to ask out of the way, we can go about our day." She poured him a cup of tea, then handed him a scone on a pretty matching plate. After taking a cup of her own, she leaned back in the couch. "Well, what is it, James?

I can assure you that you're not going to get it. So, ask so we can tell you no."

"You're not the least bit nice. I want a job like Shep here has." Harris looked at Shep, then back at his dad when he shrugged. "You can afford it. Just give me a job paying what he's making, and I'll be all right for a little while."

"Shep is going to be my husband, you moron. Even if he was working here, which he is not, I wouldn't hire you if I needed something and you were the last man on earth." Dad asked her why not. "You're untrustworthy. A pain in the ass. You abused your poor wife and children, and you're a piece of shit."

Dad stood up, and so did Shep. Harris didn't move, just continued to sip her tea like there wasn't a hostile cat standing in front of her. When she put her cup on the trolley and stood herself, she just stood there.

"If you so much as lay a hand on me, I'm going to kill you. Then I'll call the police, and since they know what sort of ass you are, they'll just cart your body away and we'll all be happy. I know I will." This time his dad looked at him. Shep just smiled at him. "If you think that he's going to mourn your passing, you're stupider than I thought you were."

A cell phone rang, and his dad screamed like she'd really shot him. It was so funny that he started laughing so hard that his father threatened him. Shep let a little of his cat go, just enough to make himself bigger.

"Touch me and they won't have to come for your body. There won't be a bit of you left when I finish with you." His dad looked around the room, probably for something to hit him with. "Go ahead, Dad. I would love for you to try to hit either of us."

105

"This is no way to treat your father. I deserve respect from you, you little fucker. All I wanted was some cash to hold me over." Harris asked him what he was holding over for. "What do you care, missy? I don't like you one bit. And as for my son marrying you, that isn't going to happen either. I rule them because I sired them. Now, you just get that shit out of your head right now."

Harris put her fingers into her mouth and let out a whistle that made his cat cringe away from it. As soon as the staff, it looked like nearly all of them, entered the room, the two security guards did as well, weapons out and ready.

"This man is Mr. Sheppard's son. He is also the father of my future husband. If he shows up here again, I want you to simply detain him. I don't care how you do it, but if he breaches the front door again, I'm going to be pissed off." Everyone nodded and said they would take care of him. "Right now I want him escorted off the property. Again, I don't care how you do it, but I want him gone. Don't kill him unless he tries to harm you, but get him out of our house."

When his dad was taken out of the house, Harris sat down, then put her head between her legs, and he went to her. She was pale when she raised her head and looked at him, and Shep asked her if she was all right.

"I hate talking to someone like that." She laughed. "Especially when I have no means of making sure that he understands that I mean business. Will he be back, Shep?"

"Yes." He sat down on the floor, rubbing his hands up and down her legs until she sat back on the couch. "He's not going to be happy when he figures out that we're getting married and — Holy shit, I forgot."

Digging into his pocket, he pulled out the little package

that he'd picked up yesterday. It was the rings that he'd had cleaned and sized for her. Putting the first ring on her finger, he told her just what he'd done with it.

"This is my mom's engagement ring. It's small, I know, but I had two more diamonds put on it for you. I've never seen it so clean and shiny. The guy who cleaned it for me said that the stains from the fruit that she put up had worked their way into the gold. I think this was my grandmother's ring before Mom got it." Shep slipped the ring onto her finger, and handed her the second ring.

"It's my mother's ring. This is so much better than just having a single ring, Shep. It's like both of the women that we loved will be with me all the time." He nodded. "Oh, look at it. I've not seen it in years. I was afraid that they'd buried her with it."

"Taylor told me that he made sure that they didn't. He also managed to get your father's ring. I have it should you want to use it." She said that she did. "I've had it cleaned too, and sized. I had hoped that you'd want to use it. Also, I put a small cut in the back—that way if I have to shift with it on, I can do so without losing a finger."

Shep handed her her father's ring, and she put the two of them together. The smaller daintier ring of her mother's fit nicely into the one that her father had worn. It was only bigger by a size for him to wear, so he thought they must have looked like the two of them when they'd been alive.

"Taylor told me that my parents' things were in the safe. I've not wanted to go and check it out yet." She looked at him. "I'm not ready for that yet either. But these things, they mean a great deal to me. Thank you so much."

"You are so very welcome. On Friday we're going to

be husband and wife. I don't think that I could have picked anyone more meaningful to me than you are." They kissed, a long lingering kiss that made his head a little light. "I love you so very much, Harrison Parker. I'm looking forward to spending the rest of my life with you, making you the happiest that I can."

"I love you too. I didn't think I'd ever find someone like you either. Loving you has come so naturally to me. I wanted to say it to you for the first time when we were married, but this is so much better." Shep told her he thought so as well. "I love you, Shep. Will you take me upstairs now? Show me just how much you love me too?"

He didn't hesitate, but stood up and picked her up in his arms. He was nearly up the stairs when the doorbell rang. Waiting for Taylor to come into the hallway, he said the elderly man's name.

"Whoever it is, the man and lady of the house are too busy to talk right now. We'll talk to them tomorrow." With a grin on his face, Taylor told them that he would tell them just that. "Thanks. And no supper tonight, but if you'll leave something in the fridge for later, that would be fine by me."

He could have sworn that he heard his butler laugh before opening the door. Shep didn't know who was there, but he sent them on their way. Just as he closed the door to their room, Shep heard the man laughing again. It was almost the best sound that he'd ever heard. Right now he was going to create the best sound by making Harris moan a few hundred times.

# Chapter 8

Harris wanted to be sexy, but she wasn't entirely sure how to do that. When Shep put her down on her feet, she made her way to the bathroom. She wasn't even sure what she was supposed to do in there, but she did put on her nightgown, then took it off. It was one of those old fashioned ones that her grandmother might have worn.

Looking in the mirror, Harris took a good look at her body. She had had scars on her, most of them from bullet wounds. A few of them were knife wounds too. But they were so tiny now that she'd taken Shep's blood that she could hardly see them anymore.

"Fuck it." Opening the door, she stood there until Shep looked at her. The man was just too good looking for his own good. As soon as he looked at her, crushing the picture frame that had been hers, she laughed. Shep smiled back at her.

"I hope that wasn't anything too important." She shook her head and started toward the bed. "No, we're going to start this right here, with you standing up."

"I'm not sure what I'm supposed to do. I know what sex is and how it works—it's not like I've never had it before. But with you, Shep, I'm sure that it'll be so different that I'll think I'm still a virgin." He told her that it would be mind blowing. "Says you. I've never even heard of anyone that has had mind blowing sex before."

"You will now." He took off his shirt and moved toward her, crawling on his all fours like a big cat. "He wants to mark you at some time. Just a bite to your thigh or calf. It won't hurt as bad as you might think. But he needs to do it."

"You talk too much." His laughter made her smile again, and when he pulled her legs apart, she moaned. The lick to her clit and his tongue going around it made her moan. He was going to drive her crazy with— "Holy Christ, yes, again."

He touched a nerve inside of her body that seemed to sizzle and ping all over her. She had to convince her feet that it was all right to uncurl her toes, it had felt so wonderful. Shep had a way with his mouth that made her beg for more one moment and then for mercy the next. Christ, he was going to kill her, and she just didn't care.

She came three times before she had to hold onto something. The only thing that was close enough for her to touch was the post of the big bed that had been delivered just today. Gripping it as hard as she could, all she could think about was that he was going to make her regret telling him that there wasn't anything like mind blowing sex.

It was like he had something to prove to her, and proving it he was. Never in all her life had she come so many times without actual sex. Harris was sure that when they got to that part, if she was still alive, she was going to be a limp, over-cooked noodle.

Shep ate at her for what seemed like hours. His mouth was all over her, his hands massaging her flesh like he was making her supple enough to eat. Harris felt her body tense up when a climax was coming, only to begin again when he would bring her to that point once again. She was dizzy with it, but knew somehow that there was more to come, and when she got it, when Shep shared it, she was going to come like the roof was coming off the house and she'd be shot to the moon.

Finally she could take no more. Begging him to let her go, he only doubled his efforts at making her scream again. When her knees were ready to give out on her, he finally let her go, but only to pick her up and take her to the bed. Limp as she'd ever been, Harris thought that she'd get to rest a little while. Boy, was she ever wrong.

Harris was sure that the little rest of ten seconds where he picked her up was all he needed to get more creative with her body. For him to renew his effort in making her dead. Even as he got on the bed with her, his hands were all over her body again.

His cock was touching her thighs as he ate at her breasts. Suckling at the tips made her wild with need. Shep massaged them as well, squeezing and holding them like he was going to make milk come from the tips. A child, her mind screamed at her. A child with this man.

"I want you." She nodded, then shook her head. "You don't want me. Well, that sucks, because I'm painfully full, and you're so ripe for me right now. Are you sure about that, honey?"

"I want a child with you. Is that possible?" Shep nodded at her, his face wearing a look of hope and love. "As soon as we can, I'd like to create a child with you, Shep. Please. I need

111

your child."

"I want that as well, but you're not in heat right now." She moaned when he slipped deep inside of her, his cock seemingly growing to fill every part her of body. "You're so beautiful, Harris. You make me want to be a better man."

"Take me."

He did too, filling her over and over as his cock moved in and out of her. The more she cried out, the faster and harder he seemed to take her, until at the very last moment, when she was ready to scream down the world around them, he stiffened over her, his back bowed back, and he cried out so loudly that she was sure that the household had heard him. Then he took her again.

Harris wrapped her legs around his, holding onto his shoulders as he pounded her hard, almost painfully. And when he bit down on her breast, making her cry out in pleasure, he fucked her harder still, bringing her to such heights that she knew that if she fell from here, there would never be another chance of coming back from this.

Her climax ripped her apart. She came with such completeness that she didn't breathe, didn't think her heart beat for several seconds. And when she came back from it, just enough to catch her breath, she came again, screaming out his name over and over until she felt his teeth scrape over her flesh and he bit into her.

There was a moment of pure clarity where she saw them. They were sitting around a tree, decorated in so many bright colors that it almost hurt. Presents were everywhere. Children too. And there, sitting next to Shep, was the most beautiful woman she'd ever seen. It was his mom.

No one could see them; she was sure of that. But his mom

was leaning over Shep's shoulder, looking at the child that he held. Her mom was there too, just on the other side, talking to Shep's mom about their grandchild. Her father was there, sitting next to the tree, watching the other children marveling at the gifts. Then in a snap of a finger she was back in her bed with Shep, and he was saying her name over and over.

"I thought that I'd killed you." She smiled up at him, touching his face with her fingers. "You were out so hard that I really thought that I'd fucked you to death."

"You might have. I saw your mother." He frowned at her. "She was with my mom and dad, and they were looking at our baby. She's beautiful, your mom. Her reddish hair pulled back into a neat bun. Her fingers so prettily stained with berries. And the most beautiful golden eyes that seemed filled with tears as she looked down at our child."

"Tell me about her face." Harris closed her eyes and thought about the woman's face. "My mom didn't wear makeup. She said that it got into her eyes when she was working. What else can you tell me about her face?"

"She has a scar on her chin. It's not all that wide, but it's long. Her ears are pierced, but she doesn't have her...wait, she does have them in. They're small. Like the size of an eraser. They're diamonds, I think." When Shep didn't say anything, Harris looked at him. "Did I say something wrong?"

"No. It was her. The earrings were from us. We pooled our money and got them for her for a Mother's Day so long ago I forgot about them. Dean ordered them, and since he had no clue what the size chart was, he ordered the biggest number they had. Of course, that turned out to be smaller. But she loved them as much as if they were sixteen carat." She asked about the scar. "It was from Dad. He lashed out with

113

her as his cat, and she never forgave him for that. It had to be stitched up because she refused to shift and have it gone. Mom said that she wanted him to see it each time he looked at her. He did too, commenting on how she should have covered it up with something. How did you see her?"

"I don't know. Perhaps it was the mind blowing sex that I had." He laughed, but he still looked nervous. "We had children around the tree, Shep. I think that this wasn't the first time that they visited, either. They seemed to be very familiar with each other."

He laid down beside her, holding her hand and looking at the ceiling. She waited; he was thinking. One thing she'd learned about Shep was that he was someone who did their thinking quietly. When he looked at her, she could see that whatever he'd thought about, it was going to be great.

"My mom would have loved you. I mean, she'd have been hitting you with her spoon every time you cursed, but she'd love you to pieces. I can see her now, knitting booties for the babies that come along." He hugged her naked body to his and she laid there, thinking that she had really ended up on the best end of life. Having a family like this to be there for her, it was something that she hadn't had before.

The two of them played around in the bed. Then in the shower too. It was nice, just having nothing to do but to be with each other. They made love again and again, and every time it got better, more romantic. Harris thought it was because the need had been lessened. Whatever it was, she was as happy as she'd ever been. In fact, Harris didn't think she'd ever been this happy in her life.

They made plans for Grandda. He needed something to do and someplace to go daily. He'd been hanging around the grocery store—Harris thought that he was sweet on one of the clerks. Thankfully he walked there and back. He did drive when he needed to, but not that often. Harris thought about hiring him a driver, someone that could cart him around when he wanted to go, but she'd have to do it without him thinking that she thought that he was old. No, he'd be hurt by that, surely.

At midnight they were both starving, so they made their way to the kitchen. There were sandwiches made up, with lettuce and tomato on the side. Several containers of salads too. She found her favorite, macaroni salad, and ate it while Shep put together the sandwiches. Tea was there, as well as beer. She had one of those while Shep drank tea. Harris asked him why he didn't drink.

"No real reason. I don't care for the taste, but it's not horrible. It would take a great deal to make me drunk, so I didn't want to waste money on that. Besides, being out on a rig, you don't want to let your guard down or you could die. There is no coming back from falling that far into an ocean."

After they cleaned up the kitchen, they dragged their asses to bed and fell asleep. She knew that she'd not be able to sleep all that late, having gotten up early all her life, but she would take a nap later in the day if she needed one. Yawning for the second time, she let sleep take her under.

~*~

Lily read the missive twice before she closed her eyes. Whatever she had thought was going on with Shelly, it certainly wasn't this. Putting away the note that had been passed to her by one of the SS, she decided that she was going to call on Harrison whenever she was feeling like someone was pulling the wool over her eyes.

Howard entered their bedroom just as she was thinking of going to find him. He worked so hard that sometimes she worried for his health. When she handed him the note, he read it just as she had. The first time with disbelief, the second time to make sure.

"She was working with the vice president in getting information? I don't want to say that she's wrong on this, but Harrison has always dug deeper than anyone that I've ever met. And while you might not like what she finds, you can bet that it's right." He got up to pace. "I wonder what she wants us to do. I can't trust the man now. Not that I ever did, but Christ, this is bad."

"I'm supposed to have dinner with Sheppard this week." He turned and looked at her, the oddest smile on his face. "What is it? Do you think he can't be trusted either? I'll have you know that that man—"

"No, I was thinking that I'd very much like to meet this paragon of manhood." He laughed. "Yes, this will be perfect. You said that he's living with Harrison and her husband?"

"Yes, but do you think that's safe, Howard? I don't want you hurt in this."

He said that if he was safe anywhere, it was at the Marshall home. "Harris is the one that trained me on how to think outside the box when it came to making myself less of a target. I wonder who it is Benson reports to. Other than me, who he is supposed to report to as my vice president. There has to be someone above him. I bet she knows."

"She more than likely does, but I doubt that she would have said anything in a note like the one she sent."

He started to pace the room. If there was a way to make this work, she knew that Howard would. Lily loved her

116

husband. It was something that she'd been teased about in the papers, how her love for him just shone through. Saps. Of course she loved him. She was supposed to, wasn't she? Morons.

"I'm supposed to go there tomorrow. There is a celebration. I'm not sure what it is, but.... Wait a minute. Codes. There's a way we can read between the lines." She took the note from him and set it on the desk she used. "All right. We got this today, and Harris would have known that. So the date is...." She wrote it down.

It was a game that she and Jill Ann used to use when they were passing notes in school. Sheppard would know it— he was the one that had taught it to them. Never once were they caught, either. The notes would be something like, *after school your father is picking us up*. But between the lines, what Sheppard called it, there would be an underlying note that would have to do with tests or boys that they liked. Lily got the first word almost as soon as she started.

"We used to use the date so that it would change daily. The month is May, so it's three letters. See? So I write down the third letter every time. If there is a space, that's a letter in the count too." She wrote them all down. Howard said it was gibberish. "Yes, it is. Until I use the date. Because it's a double digit date, we add them up. So, it's five. Now I take away each fifth thing I wrote down."

She handed the finished note to Howard. Lily was so proud of herself. *Come to wedding. There will be lots of guests that we can use. Love H.*

"How did you make this up?" She said that they'd write out the note, then work from there. It would be easier once she started using it again. "I think he was the one that fixed it

117

up for us. People don't know just how brilliant that man is."

"I guess not." She asked him if he would be able to get away. "Yes. I think it's imperative that I meet this man, don't you?"

"Yes. But I also don't want you to give things away for Harris. I mean, it might be something that she should be warned about, don't you think?" He asked her if she could send a note back to her about him coming. "I can do that. I can't believe that I had it come back to me so quickly. This will help a great many things going on, I'm betting."

It took her twenty minutes to get the note finished up. Then she sent it on its way by the service man that had brought her the note from Sheppard. She put in the note that he could call and just say yes or no. With Sheppard, who knew what the man would do? But she loved him as much as she had her own parents.

Lily didn't know when to expect a reply from anyone, so she went about her business as first lady. It wasn't until just after noon that she turned on the television to watch the game show that she was addicted to. There was breaking news on, and she watched as Shelly Main was discovered in her home, dead. Lily was also startled to realize that Shelly was the VP's daughter.

The news report said that there wasn't any sign of a break in, nor did it look as if there might be foul play involved. She had been in the shower and had fallen, it looked like. It was then said that she was the secretary for the first lady, as well as daughter to the vice president. She would be sorely missed, it said.

The reporter showed pictures of Shelly while she'd been alive. College pictures, as well as some of her as a child. Vice

President Collier could not be reached for comment. She wondered what he'd say. That he was disappointed that his daughter could no longer spy on people? That she was a good spy while it lasted? Feeling terrible for thinking such things, Lily turned off the news, no longer interested in watching it.

Lily had plenty to do as first lady. There were charity organizations that she headed, and a couple of committees that she was on. When her cell phone rang, she answered without looking at it. The harsh cursing had her pulling it away from her ear to see who was talking to her like that.

"Are you there? You deserve to be held accountable for her murder. You're the one that insisted that she take her vacation, and now look. My little girl is dead." Lily wasn't sure what to say to Benson Collier, so she kept her mouth shut. "Got nothing to say, do you? Well, I have plenty. Just wait until the newspapers find out that you sent her away and killed her."

"Benson, you're not thinking right. How could I have been responsible for her falling in the shower? And I didn't even know that she was your daughter until the news report." He said that it was murder. "I don't think anyone is going to believe you in that. She fell. And me making her take her vacation has nothing to do with that."

"You should have had her there, where she was doing good work. She was good for us, you know. All the information that she gave us was helpful on so many levels. You had no right to send her away." Lily pushed the button on her desk. It would bring her secret service men to her, and Howard if he wasn't too busy. As soon as they entered, she put the phone on speaker, and let them hear Benson screaming at her about how she'd murdered his daughter.

119

When Howard joined her, Benson was still screaming about her murdering his daughter. The men there were recording it now on their own devices, and she would only answer what they told her to say. Quietly she told Howard what had been going on since he called.

"I heard from him about an hour before they found her body. He was upset that Shelly had been sent away like she was nothing." Lily pointed out that it was unused vacation. "I know that, honey, but he's grieving, and that's what it is."

"I don't know, Howard. He said something funny to me. He told me how she was good for us, meaning him, I think. That all the information that she gave them was helpful on so many levels. What did he mean?" He said that he didn't know, but not to mention it. "No, I won't. I'll not tell anyone else. But I'll let Harris— Howard, do you think...?"

"Don't say it." She nodded as he whispered in her ear. "We'll be there in a couple of days, and we'll have some answers. If she did, then there is a good reason for it. As you've been told about, more than likely."

"All right. You're right. But what about Benson? Do you think that he's going to be trouble now?" Howard nodded. "Yes, I think so as well. Maybe we're getting ahead of this before things get too far gone."

"When what gets too far gone?" Another man that she had never trusted, the press secretary, Maron Davidson. "Benson, I don't think he's anything to worry about, do you? I mean, his little girl has just died, and he has to blame someone. All this business of you being at fault, Mrs. Steele, it's nothing to worry yourself over."

"She's the first lady, Mr. Davidson." She wanted to tell the guard not to worry about it right now, but didn't. "We have all we need, Mr. President. If you don't mind, I'd change my phone number as soon as you can. Also, I'd stay out of his line of sight for a few days. Let him cool down. I've taken steps to have someone pick him up."

"Is that necessary? As I was just telling them, he's grief stricken." The SS man, Shawn Gibson, said that it was necessary. That in order to keep everyone safe, they did not want to take any chances. "Well, it sounds to me that everyone went a little overboard on this. He's just spouting off. Let me talk to him, and I'll calm him down."

"No, I'd rather let the ones that know what they're doing talk to him. He might be grief stricken, as you say, but he just blamed his daughter's death on my wife." There was a hard tone to Howard's voice, and she moved closer to him. "Now, what is it you wanted, Davidson, that made you come into my personal home?"

"Nothing. I just saw everyone rushing here and thought I'd make sure that things were all right. Nothing to it." He smiled, but Lily could see the anger there, his disappointment in how things were going. Lily wasn't sure that Harris had killed Shelly, but she was glad now if she had. It had brought out all the anger that had been hidden before, brought it to the surface so that everyone could be aware of it. Not that she wanted the young girl dead, but things had been moving toward an end, she was sure of it. What it was going to be was anyone's guess, but she thought that however it ended, Harrison was going to be the one to end it for them.

Once everyone left, Davidson seemed to linger a little too long, asking questions too of the security team, like when were they going to pick up Collier. What they were planning to do with him. All the while, they never answered him, and at one point, Shawn asked him to state his business. He looked at her when she moved near the doorway to give him the hint that she wanted him out of their home.

"I'm sure that once you think about things, you'll understand that he meant you no harm." She asked him why he thought that. "Because he's a good friend of mine, and you have to see that he's been dealt a hard blow. I'd just call them all off, and I'm sure in a couple of days he'll call you up and tell you how sorry he is."

"Will you make him do that, Davidson?" She didn't know where the question came from, but once she asked, she decided that she wanted an answer. "Will you make him call me up and tell me that he meant nothing by calling me a murderer? How about that it was my fault she was dead because I had her take her vacation time that was coming to her? What will you have him say to me about that?"

"I don't know what you're talking about, and I'm betting that you don't either. It could be bad for you to go making accusations like that with nothing to back it up with." He looked at her hard now, like he was looking for some way that she might have what he didn't want her to have. Information came to mind. Or deals. Lily stared back just as hard. "You aren't as tough as you think you are."

"And you aren't as smart as you believe yourself to be either. Get out, right now, before I have you escorted out of here." He leaned into her, just enough where she could smell alcohol on his breath. "In the future, don't come here unless invited, and try very hard, if you ever are invited, not to smell like you've only just came from a bar."

When she slammed the door after he finally left, she leaned back against it. She was shaking so badly that she ended up on the floor rather than trying to walk to her table. Christ, she thought, she felt like she'd only just tangled with a tiger. When her phone rang, she was almost afraid to answer. But seeing Jill Ann's face there, Lily answered it.

"Hello, my dear. I was just thinking about— What is it? What's happened?"

She started crying. Lily could hear his voice behind her sobs. He was offering her comfort and telling her that he was going to come there, but she finally calmed down enough to talk to him.

"I just was having a bad day. I'm all right now." He said that he could tell, and if she needed him, he was there. "No, no, that's all right. I hope to be seeing you soon. Did you get my message?"

"I did. Thank you, my dear. I wasn't sure you'd gotten mine." He laughed. "Yes, everything is set for you to come see us. We have a few more guests then we were planning, but the more the merrier. Yes, the more the merrier."

"Thank you so much. I cannot wait to talk to you again. You have no idea how much it helps me with the passing of my friend. She was such a wonderful person. I know you're aware of that, but I do think it was the best balm for me." He told her that they'd talk about old times, just the two of them. "Yes, I'd like that. I have some pictures too that I'm going to bring. I've dug them out of storage, if you can believe that."

"Yes, I've been finding things that I want to share with you too. You don't realize how much junk you collect until you have to go sorting through it. My wife, she had some stuff stored away for our grandboys that I'm giving them now that they have their own homes." He spoke to someone there with him, and she smiled. It must be Harris, whose foul mouth she'd heard so much about. The language was crude and funny. "Well, I've been told that you have a country to run and that I'll see you soon. I miss you, Lily child. So much."

Lily felt so much better after talking to him. After taking care that she had all the things that she wanted to take, she had herself a lying in. Sometimes in order to get her ducks in a row, she simply had to take a little nap. Lying down, she knew that she'd feel much better in a little while. Trying her best not to think of anything, she closed her eyes. In less than twenty-four hours she'd be someplace she could be free. And Lily could not wait.

# Chapter 9

"What the ever loving fuck is wrong with you?" Maron didn't like this one bit. Sure Benson's daughter had died, and it was a tragedy, but it wasn't worth putting everything that they'd worked for out there in the open like this. "How the fuck did you figure that blaming the president's wife was going to be low key?"

"She had something to do with it—I know it." Maron asked him how that was possible. "She hired someone to kill her off. Don't you think it's suspicious that two days after she made my little girl take her vacation, she fell in the shower? A little too pat, don't you think? I mean, why did she do that anyway? Shelly was doing a great job with messing with her schedule, and telling us when she was doing things outside of the house so we could keep tabs on her."

"Did the first lady just decide to go all the way across town and trip your daughter while she was in the shower? Not likely, if you ask me. Besides, if you remember correctly, you told me yourself that Shelly was drinking a little more than she should have been. And the night before she was found, didn't she go to a party being held at the local college?" Benson nodded, but said that Lily still had something to do with it. "You're just nuts. And if you keep this up, you're going to fuck things up for the two of us too."

"He's not going to suddenly decide that I'm not worthy of him talking to me about his personal life. What little personal life that he has. Christ, he's the most boring man that I've ever had to be around. Much less work with." Benson sniffled a little more. "She was my only child, Maron. Can't you understand that?"

"I can. I'm sorry for your loss, I really am. But you have to keep your mouth shut. What did you say to Lily before I got there? Christ, you didn't just blab about everything, did you?" He said that he'd not said a word about what they were doing. "I certainly hope not. That would be bad for the two of us when it comes out about the president."

The president was going to go down soon, and they were going to reap the benefits of it. Benson would be president, of course. Then Maron would be the vice president, because Benson would choose him as his second. It would be wonderfully perfect when all was said and done. They'd have everything they ever wanted, and all the money they could stash away.

They had so many people waiting for the day to happen too. Money deals that were on hold. Deals that would bring them to war almost as soon as the I do's were said. Not that they were getting married, but they would be sworn in. He looked at the list that he had on his personal phone, and wondered if it would be too risky to move things up a few more days. It seemed to be taking forever for them to get the goods in the right place for it to happen. Drugs and money would be found as soon as — Fuck. Shelly couldn't place them anymore.

While she'd been able to stash away some of the drugs that he'd stolen, the money had been a bit more problematic. It seemed to slip through his fingers at every turn. Benson had thought about counterfeit money, but so long as it wasn't circulated, then it would do them little good. Not to mention fingerprints on it.

The real money would have so many prints on it that it wouldn't matter if they couldn't find his on there. But new money, just printed up, real or not, wouldn't work. They needed the stick of the prints being traced back to Howard. No prints on them would take the blame from him and put it on someone else. Asking him to touch the money wouldn't work because the fucker would want to know why.

"Do you have any idea how many problems you're causing me, Howard?" He wouldn't care, that was what pissed him off. And his little wife Lily was pissing him off as well. "She had her little feelings hurt by Benson, and had to call in the national guard."

She'd not done that, but just as bad. Calling the secret service in was like calling in the army, navy and air force all at one time. Christ, he wished he'd been with Benson when he found out about his daughter. Then he could have knocked him around a little before he decided to make a call that would come back to bite them in the ass.

"What are you mumbling about?" He'd forgotten that Benson was with him when he started bitching under his breath. "You don't think that they had a thing to do with it, do you?"

"No, I don't." He asked about Cora Banks, the hit man that worked for the government. "Yes, that would be her MO, but she's dead. I have told you this over and over. Did she resurface after that thing we sent her on? No, she didn't. And do you know why she didn't? Tell me Benson, why didn't she?"

"Because you killed her." He smiled at the man. "What about her paperwork? You said that it had to be done after she was dead. What happened to her file, Maron?"

"I don't care. It was blank. I supposed that's what it was when she was hired on for what she does. And there is no telling how long it had been that way." It did bother him about her file. There was a picture in it, but when he was looking over it, someone next to him said they had the same picture in their new wallet. Then he showed him. "You just let me worry about whether or not she's alive. She's dead to you, that's all you have to worry about."

If she was alive, however, they were going to be in a world of hurt. Not only would she come after them, but she'd make sure that they were dead too. No one would ever suspect that she had anything to do with it either. She was that good. Damned good is what he'd heard about her.

After leaving Benson to his bed — they had brought him to the hospital when he'd freaked out — Maron went home. His house was bug free, so he didn't even bother trying to keep anything hidden away there. Pulling out his phone, he made a call to his contact that had told him about Cora being dead.

"I have been looking for her body since you called me." He asked him why he'd not found it. "I don't know. I followed her until the marketplace, then she was gone. I think she had people helping her."

"Of course she did. But when I called you before, you assured me that she was not only dead, but that you'd seen the body." He said that he'd lied—just that he'd lied. Then he laughed. "I don't fucking think this is funny at all, you moron. I want you to find her body, and find it now. Christ, do you have any idea what this will do to us if she's not dead?"

"It won't bother me." The giggle again, and Maron wanted to climb through the phone and kill the little fucker. "I've nothing to do with her. Dead or alive? It matters very little to me."

"I'm going to kill you." The man laughed again before he hung up. Calling him back did him no good either—the line, the operator said, was no longer in service. "Mother fuck."

He nearly threw the phone across the room, but stopped at the last moment. His butler would murder him if he did that again, and he didn't need any more staff leaving him at the moment. As it was, he was having to pick up his own dry cleaning and pick out his shirts. Maron was used to the finer things in life, and having only two people working for him in a house this size wasn't cutting it.

He saw no reason to hire anyone else when he'd be moving soon. To the VP house, reserved for men like him. Maron had an idea that he'd piss a few people off when he was living there, but they could suck a big cock for all he cared. He was going to be making things happen with his best bud, and then they'd sit up and take notice of him.

Getting his tux out, he was pissed because it was the wrong one. There was no way that he'd put on that much weight between the last time he'd worn it and now. He yelled for the butler to see if he had picked up the right one when he heard a voice behind him. Then it was in front of him, saying his name over and over. Finally taking out his gun, Maron demanded that whoever it was show themselves. The woman that came out of the darkness nearly had him wetting his pants.

"I heard that you're looking for me." He just shook his head, not sure that he could speak when he saw how she was dressed. And there was no doubt at all that this person was a she. Christ, her black on black outfit fit her like a glove. Maron could see her eyes and nothing more. "Well, what is it you want, Maron? I'm a busy woman."

"I don't know who you are." The gun came out of someplace in her outfit, and was pointed right at his head. He could feel it there like she was trying to make him a weird sort of art project that had to do with guns and brains. "Don't kill me."

"Not yet, I won't. Do you know who I am?" He nodded. "Good. Then we can skip over the pleasantries. You're not going to find my body, in the event that you didn't get that."

"Cora Banks." She did a little bow at him, and he wanted her to fucking die where she stood. "You're very difficult to get in touch with, you know that? I have a job for you."

"No you don't. You just wanted to know if I was dead or not. Now that we've established that I'm not, tell me what you're up to." He asked her if she'd killed Shelly Main. "Did I? Hmm, I haven't any idea what you're talking about. But if I did, it was because she was stashing coke all over the White House in order for you and your buddy to get the president impeached. Is that about right?"

"Why would I do something like that?" She turned her back to him and he didn't move. All he needed was to get himself laying in the bed next to Benson. "How the hell did you get in here?"

"The front door. How did you think I'd get into your home? I've been in your buddy's house too. Too bad about him, however." He asked her if she was going to go to the hospital and harass him. "Not unless I don't get the answers I want from you. What is the big plan between you guys? Besides getting the president into trouble."

"Benson isn't going to be causing any more troubles for me, so you just stay the fuck away from him. His daughter was just murdered. By you. What do you think he's going to do when he finds out that you did it?" She paused for a moment, then turned back to him. "You did kill her, didn't you?"

"Like you, I don't know what you're talking about." She stood by the window that he had never opened since he'd been in this house. It was blowing cool night air in as he stood there.

"You know that there are cameras all over this place, don't you? Not only will it tell me how you got into my home, but it will show that you threatened me as well."

"I'm not worried about your cameras. You shouldn't either if you know what's good for you. So you and Collier are in on this, are you?" Maron had a second of clarity. She hadn't known what his partner's name was until he'd told her. "If Benson is as stupid as you are, I'm not going to have too much trouble exposing you, am I? Christ, you guys get dumber every time I have to deal with one of you. So drugs, and I'm thinking money. You're going to stash them all over his personal residence, then put out a tip. It won't work, you know. On so many levels. But you're not going to be able to make that stick, because I've taken care of things. Things do not seem to be going in your favor right now, Maron. Whatever will you do?"

"I don't know what you're talking about." Her laughter made him think of bells atop a church that rang on Easter morning. It was soft and lyrical. Pretty even. He had a feeling that while this woman had a great body—he could see every curve of her—her face was something that his brother used to call Butter Face. She'd be pretty butter face was ugly. "I want you out of here right now."

"I'm leaving. One more thing before I leave, however. You should stop now. If I have to come back here, neither one of you are going to make it to the next sunrise. You can count on that." He said he wasn't afraid of her. "Yes you are, Maron. You're so close to wetting your pants that I can almost smell you."

She raised her head up and sniffed loud enough for him to hear her. Then she simply disappeared out the window. Running to see where she'd gone, he forgot to worry that she might be right there. She wasn't.

There wasn't a trace of her around. Not in the garden below, nor in the tree that was just too close to his home for comfort now. Pulling out his gun, he thought about just firing up in the tree to kill her, but he knew she wouldn't be hit. His luck wasn't that good.

The noise behind him had him turning and firing at the same time.

"Mother fuck."

He'd just killed his butler.

~*~

Shep watched her pace back and forth. Whatever had happened when she'd been out, it had pissed her off enough that she couldn't even speak to him. So far all he'd gotten from her was that the vice president was in on this.

"They were sending Collier's daughter in to hide evidence around the personal home of the president and his wife. And if that wasn't bad enough, the drugs that were there had been stolen from evidence rooms all over the DC area. They still had the stations markings on them." She paced more. The room that they'd rented here was in his name. They had spent last night here, and were leaving today. "I'm glad that I went over the place today and not later. There is no telling how much more stuff would have been added to the household before I got there."

"Did you kill Shelly?" She nodded. "You said that she was into some serious shit. Can you tell me what it was? I don't want to be blindsided about that tomorrow when we talk to Mr. and Mrs. President."

"Gathering things. Like their fingerprints to use on other things, stolen things. DNA too. Things like hairs from Lily's brush. Pubic hair from the shower that he used. There were missing pictures too. I found those at the apartment when I was there. She was cropping them with females to make it look like he was having a gang banger with prostitutes." Harris turned and looked at him. "She had enough ammo and other guns there that she could have been ready for a war no problem. The dig is, I don't think her dad or Maron even knew about the guns."

Shep didn't even know how that sort of thing could be done with fingerprints and taking things from brushes. And pubic hair? That was just not even right. The pictures, he'd seen that done. But the rest, no.

"What are you going to tell them when they get there?"

Shep picked up the luggage when she went into the bathroom to change and gather the things she'd left in there. When she came out, she had on a pretty sun dress and sandals. Nothing like the woman she'd been when she left him earlier. "I think that is why you're so very good at what you do. No one would suspect you of being a hit man."

"That's the point, yes. I'm having trouble wrapping my head around the VP being a part of this. I'm going to have to think on this hard about what they're planning. I mean, I've figured out that they're going to take over the presidency, but after that, I don't know. Well, I do have a clue, but I don't want that to be it." He asked her what it was. "War. And a huge one too. All they need to do is push the right people into the wrong places, and there will be a war that will kill everything that this country has worked for."

As soon as they left the hotel room, they headed for the car. Driving back and using cash left very little footprint, she'd told him. Shep had a lot of television knowledge about crimes, so knew a little about why she had him doing this. It meant that they were less likely to be traced. And even though the hotel had his name for staying there, she'd taken care of the computers so that no one would know what he looked like, when he came or went, and most importantly, if Shep had anyone in the room with him. They'd not even know that he ordered two of each meal that they'd had there. She was that good.

The ride home was made with him doing the listening. When she talked to him, it was mostly to vent, he supposed. And when she did ask him a question, he was never sure if she was asking or venting again. Shep just kept his mouth shut.

He was very proud of her, to be honest, the way that she worked things out in her head and then tossed them out like they were solid. They sounded that way to him. But she'd find a flaw in it someplace and start again. What he did get out of all this was that both men would have to be killed. There wasn't any way that she could just let them go to prison over this. It would be a nightmare to get them tried, as well as sentenced. They had too many people in their pockets.

"I have to make sure that they're both killed at the same time, too. If I do one then the other, people will start asking questions. Questions that I do not want to answer." Shep was sitting right next to her, listening to every word, and didn't think he'd be able to answer anything either. "I think that if I have to do them one at a time, Benson is going to be a victim of not being able to live without his poor daughter. Maron, however, when he goes, he is going to suffer big time. That fucker makes me sick."

"You know something about him, don't you?" She nodded and he waited. When nothing was forthcoming, he finally asked. "Do I want to know what you do, or can I just assume that when he goes it's going to be justified?"

"Oh, it'll be justified. Right now it's treason, conspiracy, and a whole lot of other things. He's threatened the wife of the sitting president. Made threats against the country. Oh yeah, it'll be justified." Shep asked if there was something else. "Yes. He's been dealing with drugs that come from overseas. Not like pot or other things like that, but ecstasy. So far I've linked three deaths with his brand. The idiot didn't even come up with a name for it that would keep him out of it. It's actually called *Davidson's fuck*. It's written in a different language, so it's doubtful that anyone else caught it."

"I see." He did too. The man was supposed to be taking care of our country, and here he was making money off the deaths of others. He did deserve to die. "I wish I could help you with this. I mean, even in a small way, I wish I could."

"You are. All the time. Because of you, I didn't kill them both when I had the chance. And believe me, I've had them. But here's the thing. I don't want to fuck this up for Lily and Howard. I don't know them that well, but your grandda does, and he really likes Lily. I want him to be happy with the outcome of this too." Shep was happy that she said that. His grandda did love Lily. "We'll be able to talk to them tomorrow, so I'll get some answers then. If not, then I don't know what we'll do."

The rest of the drive was made with just small talk. They had fun, driving through the night and getting home. Twice they stopped for gas, and got some snacks to go with their drinks. Once home, they nearly didn't make it up the stairs, they were both so exhausted.

In the morning they were going to be married. Shep was glad that they'd been able to pull that off. Even with the ad in the paper, no one would know who they were. Parker was a common enough name, and he wasn't really into the same circles as people the Parkers might have hung out with.

Getting up the next morning, he found himself alone in his bed. He'd really expected that. The groom wasn't to see his bride before the big event anyway. Shep wished that his mom were here today. It would have made her so happy to know that he was getting married, and to someone that he was proud to call his wife. She would have loved Harris too. Mom might have been a little scared of her. Then maybe not, he thought. His mom had been pretty kick ass too.

Dressing in his tux, Shep went down the stairs to the first level of the house. It had been decorated. There were flowers and balloons everywhere. Even a wedding cake was being assembled in the kitchen for them. Also, there were small sandwiches, as well as punch. Grandda came out of the living room just as he was going through the room because all the furniture was missing.

"I had it stored up for you. I thought that this room would make a nice dance floor. What do you think?" He hugged the older man, and then hugged him again. "I surely wish my Jill Ann was here. Your grandma too. They would have had a good time today. Showing off their new member of this family."

"I was thinking the same thing this morning. Mom would have been right in there with Harris, making sure that she got the bad guys. Dad would have been barred not only from the day, but ever coming around again. She'd have wanted things to be perfect." Grandda sniffled, and Shep held him a little longer. "Grandda, I'm so very glad that you're here with us. I don't mean just today, but I mean here all the time. I know that the others, they like having you around too."

"Your little miss, she asked me to give her away. I never felt so good in my life. I had to go right over and tell the women folk about it. I have to tell you, Shep, I no longer feel like I have to stay there all day to be with her. I got all you here, and that is enough for me." He wiped his nose with his ever present handkerchief, then put it away. "I miss them both, but I'm feeling better every day."

"Me too, Grandda." He didn't mention his dad. Dad wasn't going to be allowed here, and he was fine with that. Dad had made his bed, now he had to lie in it.

137

His brothers showed up and he knew that something had happened to Oakley. When Oakley told him that he'd tell him later, it was all he could do not to rip off his shirt and see why he was holding his ribs. Dad. He didn't know why, but he knew that Dad had caught him off guard and hurt him. Other guests started to arrive—they'd not invited that many—and he had to leave Oakley to his pain. But he swore to Christ that he was going to take care of their father once and for all. Enough was enough, damn it.

At a quarter to eleven, the Steeles, Howard and Lily, showed up. They looked so happy to be there that he found himself in a better mood simply from being around them. He had met Lily, of course, but meeting the president was something that he never in all his life thought would happen. Talking to them, he thought one would never know that they were the president and his wife.

When the music began, he went to stand up by the beautifully decorated trellis that was just outside of the house on the lawn. When he saw Harris coming toward him on his Grandda's arm, he nearly wept. She was dressed in an off white dress that he was sure was older than her. The closer she got, he could see that it was his mother's dress. Someone, probably Grandda, had dug it out for her and had it fitted. Harris looked like a dream to him. He fell in love with her all over.

Kissing her as soon as Grandda handed her off, the crowd of people laughed. As the words were said over them to make them husband and wife, he nearly forgot to say I do, he was so enthralled by the beauty before him. Before he realized it, they were pronounced man and wife, and Harrison Elizabeth Parker Marshall was his bride.

He spoke to Oakley finally. Dad had caught him off guard as he had thought, and hit him with a bat in the ribs before Oakley turned the tables. Oakley only had to shift and he'd be fine. Shep was glad for that.

# Chapter 10

Harris could tell that Howard was overwhelmed by the information that she'd given him. Every time he started to ask a question, he'd just stop and not say anything. She thought what had really gotten him was the fact that they both wanted to start a war. Just when everything in the country was starting to look up.

"That could be the reason, sir. They're not making as much money as they would be if they were into a war. Guns to be transferred around. Then there is food and clothing that could be stolen only to be resold. These men have been at this for a while, and they know the ropes." He looked at her with pleading eyes, and she stopped talking for a moment. At least about the two men out to get him out of office. "Thank you for the wedding gift. It was very nice of you to bring one."

"We didn't bring a gift and you well know it. But I do thank you for letting me have a breather. This thing with Shelly. She was in with them, I guess." Harris told Howard what she'd found when she'd gone to the house. "We had thought that you were the one that had somehow killed her. I didn't want to know, as you can guess, but Lily and I had it figured out. What sort of guns did you find there?"

After handing him the list of them that she'd stored away, Harris handed him the key to the storage locker that she'd put them in. Howard handed them back to her, telling her that she was better equipped to hide them than he was.

"There's more — are you ready for it?" He told her that he didn't think so, but for her to tell him. "There are drugs and guns coming across the borders that are marked for them. I haven't found the storage units that they're holding them in, but I have a tag on one of the trucks that is coming in."

"What sort of tag are you talking about? One that we can trace from here?" Harris told him that she'd rather not mention it just yet. So she could work out the details. "I don't want you anywhere near to these men. I don't want you hurt."

"Sir, this is my job, to take out the bad guy. I've been doing this since before you were the president. I'm really good at it. They'll never know that it's me. My file has been fucked with, and once they get around to pulling it — I'm sure they will soon, if not already — they'll see nothing that I didn't want them to see." He asked her what that might be. "Nothing. There is a fake picture that I got from someplace. Blank sheets of paper that are supposed to be my information. Oh, and the note that I left them. It simply tells them that I'm much smarter than they will ever be."

"You are. Why is it you don't work for me?" She said she did, that he was the one that signed her paycheck each month. "I don't think that we're paying you nearly enough for all that you do. I've been going over some old newspapers, and I think you've been doing more for this country than I have.

142

Thank you for that."

"No problem. I sort of like it here." They both laughed, and she handed him the last of the information that she had for him. "I killed Shelly, as you are aware. And I'm going to kill the other two as well."

"Why not bring them to trial?" She told him. "I see. Yes, I can see where it would show me in a bad light. To have something like this going on behind my back and people thinking that they can take advantage of me. Yes, thank you for that. Do I want to know how you're going to do it?"

"Nope." She didn't say any more, and he seemed to understand. "I will need to speak to you when this is finished. I've set up my home as a command center, and before you leave, I'd like to not only take a look at your cell phones, but give you something that can tell you if there are bugs in any of the rooms you live in."

"They're swept daily." She didn't have to remind him who it was he was dealing with. "Okay, yes, I'll take that too. It's funny how you can assume that things are going along just fine, only to find out that you have not only a knife in your back, but a gun pointed at your head too. I wouldn't have thought this of Benson when we were first paired together. Now I'm thinking of all sorts of things that should have clued me in to what he was up to."

"I didn't know Benson was in on it until Maron told me. I knew that he had a partner, but not him. It took me a while to figure it out too. If Benson becomes president, he can choose his VP. He'll bring Davidson on board for that. With the two of them in office, it'll be a nightmare for everyone. Including anyone that supported you."

"You're talking about the house or the country." She told

him both. "I guess you're right, but I really hate to think of anyone being that terrible. To people that pay their salary."

"There are all kinds of shits in the world, sir. You know that better than most." She watched his face. He was less overwhelmed, but no less upset about things going on around him. "You need someone in your office that you can trust. Someone that can tell you when you're being fucked over and taken to the woodshed. Not as a running mate, but someone that can say, 'Hey, so and so is planning your death off a fifty-story building, you'd better fucking get him out of your life.' And soon."

"Do you ever think about what rolls off your tongue before saying it?" He looked like he thought his question was funny, so she pretended to think about it. "I see your mind working. You're trying to figure out a way for you to tell me to get my fucking head on straight before someone puts a bullet in it."

"Pretty much." They both laughed and she stood up. "I have to mingle, and so should you. This house is safer than your rooms at home. Take the device that I give you and the man that I send home with you, and use them like you would a whore on Saturday night. You don't have much choice in the matter, sir. Do it, or you will be killed or worse."

"What could be worse?" She told him that his wife could be killed and he'd have to watch. "Yes, that would be worse. Thank you for this. And while I don't really think that I'd use a whore any night of the week, I get what you're saying."

They both walked around the rooms that had been set up for the wedding party. There were guards all around the rooms too. They stood out like they were supposed to, so that anyone that entered any room knew that they were being watched and that a bullet would be used to stop anything untoward going on. She had trained these men. To her, they were as loyal as she was to the Marshall family.

There wasn't a dinner, but finger foods had been put around the room on different tables. Her and Shep would walk by each other every once in a while and hug and kiss. They were working the crowd, and it was sort of fun to see him at work. Harris wondered if Shep had any idea how much people respected him. Doubtful. Shep was a man who didn't care what people thought about him. He did as he pleased when he wanted. She loved that about him as well.

Toby Wayne knew that he was going to go to the White House when the president left here. He also had a list of phone numbers to call if the shit hit the fan. Toby was the best she'd seen at seeing outside the box. He was even better at hand to hand combat, as well as using a gun. She would trust him over a great many other people when it came to thinking of ideas and plans.

Allison Wayne, his sister, was going back with Lily to be her secretary. Allie, as she went by, was also good in hand to hand, and could use a knife like an extension of her hands. She'd be good for the first lady in that she was going to teach her things to keep her safe if she found herself alone and in trouble. It was the only way that Harris knew to keep them from being harmed while they were away from her.

"This box was specially made for me. All you have to do is set it in a room, any room, and it will tell you if you're being recorded or taped at any time. You already have one in every room of your place, and it's been swept by my team. Allison will do the same every day after your guys sweep, and this device needs to be put into the oval office with you.

I didn't want to take the chance of getting in there and being trapped. It's well guarded, but the wrong people are being let in." Howard nodded and looked at the small device before taking it. "It will emit a sound that Toby can hear. The same with the ones in the upper levels. They're wolves, so they'll hear it before you will, and will tell you about it."

"I'm afraid, if you want the truth. I don't want to go back until things are cleared up." She said she was on that. "I know you are. Christ, I'm glad that you're on my side, but that doesn't make me any less afraid of what shit they're going to try and pull."

"They're going to think they have you right where they want you. They don't. Not only that, but they think that I know a great deal more than I do. Which, to be honest with you, is very little compared to what I think is out there." He nodded and said that wasn't helping. "No, I doubt that it is. But I do know you well enough to know that you're a man that can think quickly and well when pressured. Just listen to Toby, sir. He will be the only thing between you and an obit in the paper."

"You and that truthful tongue. Perhaps you need to come up with a few lies, just to make someone feel better." Harris told him that he'd never trust her if she did that. "Probably not. No, I probably wouldn't. You'll have my back in all this, right?"

"Yes. All sides of you. Just do what I tell you. Even if it goes against everything that you believe in, I want you to do it." He nodded and said he'd try. "No. If you're only going to try, then the battle is lost. You have to do it. It might make you feel wrong, but you have to trust me that I only have your best interest in mind. Just keep your head up and pay attention to things around you. You'll start to see things that you didn't before, but don't deal with them. Leave that to me."

"All right. I'll do whatever you tell me." Howard looked at Toby, and the man just looked like your everyday nerd, from the ill-fitting shirt to the jeans that had a couple of holes in them. "I'm assuming that looks can be deceiving with you."

Toby nodded and lifted his arm, and flexed the muscles that were hidden under the shirt. It was then that you could see every muscle and bulge in his biceps. Toby knew what he was doing, giving the people around the president the illusion that he was nothing more than a pushover. But he was, as a matter of fact, a registered killer. His body was lethal.

"You remember the old saying, don't you? Keep your friends close and your enemies closer? In this case, it couldn't be more true. We will get through this if you just pay attention and listen." He said that he would. "Good. You and Lily will live a long life if you just do what you're told when they tell you. I swear to you, there isn't anyone that is going to get by these two unless they are killed protecting you."

"I don't want it to come to that." She told him that neither did she. "When this is done, I do want you to come and work for me at the White House. I could use someone like you."

"No. I can't, nor would I want to do that. I have a life here. A family that I want to start. When you are no longer in trouble, I will step down as your hired guns. I can't do that anymore and have the kind of life I want. You understand." He said that he did. "Good. I'm going to hold you to that."

After everyone left, her and Shep sat in the living room on a couple of outdoor chairs. They were both exhausted, and still needed to take care of a couple of things around the house. Mainly to clean up. Just as she was going to tell him that she'd take this room, Grace and the rest of the staff came in and shooed them off to bed.

Harris was glad for it. She needed a four day nap really bad, and she thought that she might just get it. Dragging her ass up the stairs, she screamed when Shep picked her up in his arms.

"I love you, Mrs. Marshall." She kissed him and told him that she loved him as well. "Good. I love you so much that I'm going to let you sleep tonight. Because right now, I'm going to be lucky if I get the covers over me before I fall asleep too."

They were both laughing when they entered their room. The bed was turned down and there was a bottle of champagne in an ice bucket. Falling on the first and ignoring the second, they were both asleep in about ten seconds, Harris thought.

# Chapter 11

Shep's cock felt warm, hard and painful. When he opened his eyes, he saw the most glorious sight he'd ever seen—his beautiful naked wife sitting on his cock and riding him. This, he thought, he could wake up to every day and never be a sad person ever.

"You were so hard that I just couldn't resist taking advantage of you." Shep told her that she could take him anytime she wanted. "I will hold you to that. You're so hard like this. I never knew that riding a horse could be so much fun."

He pulled her down for a kiss, eating at her mouth like he had her pussy before. Christ, she tasted like heaven, and he was wondering how much longer he could last with her there. Putting his hands on her hips, he held her to him as she rode him, grinding her pussy along his groin so that she would cry out every time she did it.

When he knew that he was close, Shep rolled her to her back. Since her legs were already around him, he moved up her body and took her with her feet up over his shoulders. He knew that he was as deep as he could go, but Harris begged him for more.

"I love the way you're fucking me. I love that you're so deep. Take me harder, Shep. I want to feel you everywhere in my body." He pounded her hard, knowing full well that she was going to be sore when he finished. And when she dug her nails into his back, he cried out. Not with pain, but with the pleasure of it. The nothing-held-back way that she screamed his name when she released.

"Again." She shook her head hard, telling him that she couldn't handle it anymore. "Yes, you can. Come for me, love, and when you do, my cat will take his bite of you and mark you as his own."

She came screaming again. The way his cat ran along his skin made him realize how much his cat was enjoying this too. Not fucking her — he'd never do that — but the unbridled way that she accepted him into her life. His cat loved her as much as Shep did.

As soon as he released, Shep pulled from her. His cat took him quickly, much quicker than he'd wanted. Shep had wanted to warn Harris that he was coming for her, but before he could stop him, the cat bit down hard on her thigh.

This time her screams were of pain. Begging the cat to back off, he felt his jaws unclamp just a little, but the blood, venous blood, filled his mouth. He'd bitten into her vein. It was finish the job or lose her to blood loss. As she begged him to stop, that he was hurting her, Shep assured her that they were going to have to change her and that she'd be all right.

It was a lie. He was sure that he'd already lost her, and was working hard on not showing how terrified he was that he might have hurt her badly. The second bite was in her belly. Harris had stopped begging him to not hurt her anymore. She'd was out cold, and he wasn't sure whether to be happier about that or more afraid. He couldn't lose her.

He could taste her better with the belly bite. Taste the fact that she had a bit of something else inside of her. It wasn't much, but enough. Shep was sure that was what gave her the gift of being able to manipulate cameras and computers.

Taking back his body, he watched her breathing. It was slow, and her heart rate was nearly nothing. It was there, very slowly beating, but he didn't know for how long. Christ, he thought, he'd just murdered the best thing in his life. The longer he sat there, watching every breath she took, Shep was happy. But he kept waiting for the one that would be her last.

Harris continued to breathe slowly. Her heartrate, while it didn't slow, was very faint. He held her hand and told her over and over how much he loved her.

"Don't die on me, love. Please? I don't know what I'd do without you. I will be worse than my grandda. I will die if you leave me. Please, you have to come back to me." He kissed her forehead and realized how cold she was. Sobbing, he laid down beside her and held her to him to keep her warm. Shep wasn't sure what else he could do.

He must have falling asleep at some point, because when he woke, he was alone in the big bed. Getting up, startled by all the blood that was on the sheets, he ran to the bathroom. Slipping on the rug, he hit his head on the counter and blacked out.

"Will you please get your ass up off my robe? I swear to Christ, if our children are this clumsy, I'm going to be really pissed off at you." He heard Harris's voice, and while the words were mean, he could hear the humor in her voice. "Sheppard James, if you do not wake up this minute, I'm going to find my gun and make you have a real reason for not waking up right now."

"Are you going to be this mean to our children when they fall and hurt their knees?" He opened one eye and looked at her, then opened the other. "Christ, you're beautiful. Have I told you that lately?"

"No." She flipped him to his belly, and left him lying there while she went into their bedroom. He watched her as she gathered up some clothing to put on. He was sort of partial to her being naked, but he decided now was not the time to be bringing things like that up. She did seem pissed right now. He asked her what had happened. "Maron is in jail. Manslaughter. I know that I should be happy about that, but I'm not. He's out of commission, but I want him out where he can get himself killed. Mainly by me. This will come back and haunt him for a long time, however."

"Who did he kill?" She told him that his butler was found dead on the floor with a sheet over him. "Why did he kill him?"

"He said that Cora Banks made him do it." It took Shep a second to remember who she was. "Yeah. I guess the butler came into the room after I left and startled him. At least that's what he's saying."

"Like you said, he's out of commission for a while." She was dressed and looked like she was leaving him there. "Wait a minute and I'll join you. I have stuff to do today too."

"You're bleeding, by the way. And how do I explain that the sheets looked like we murdered someone on them? I'm sure the staff will be appalled by it." He just smiled at her.

"You're not as charming as you might think you are right now."

"You're a cat." She asked him if he was serious. "Yes. I rarely tell a joke well, so I don't bother. Anyway, you're a jaguar, just like me. Well, not like me. I'm a boy cat, and you're so very not one."

"I don't like you right now. What do you mean, I'm a cat? I thought that I heard someplace that it took like a week for the human to be down." He told her that she wasn't wholly human. "Yes, I am. Or I was until you got all teethy on me."

"Teethy? Well, that's a new one. But yes, I did bite you. You aren't human. I mean, you weren't — This is too confusing. You're a cat, I'm a cat. I don't know what you were before this except not all human. I think that's why you can mess with computers and cameras. I would think that you're either part vampire, which I have no idea why I think that, or faerie. That would explain a lot too. The fact that you were able to get up so quickly after I changed you. Also that you seem to bounce back quickly when you're hurt."

"Okay, I can see that, I guess. Does it matter what I am in addition to being a cat? And what the hell does that have to do with the sheets and being able to explain them to the staff?" He'd forgotten about the first question, and told her. "So Grace and the rest of our staff are not human. I think that I knew a couple of them weren't, but not Grace. So, she'll know that I've been changed. She'll know what happened."

They were leaving the room then, and he was telling her that she'd be able to tell what other shifters were too. She asked why he'd thought vampire.

"I don't know, really. But that's what I'm leaning toward. It must have been a very old one to have been able to pass

153

anything down to you. I mean, it could have been anyone in your family as far back as the beginning of vampires. I don't know any, do you?" She told him that she knew two vampires. "Good. Perhaps you can ask one of them sometime to see if they could bite you and tell who you might be related to."

"Is it important? I mean, to you?" He said that it wasn't, but it might be to the vampire or his descendants to know that someone out there was carrying the line along. "Oh. Well, I'll talk to them when this is done. Okay, for today, I need to go and visit Maron. He doesn't know me as my real self, so I have to think of something as a reason to go and see him."

"You could be the butler's daughter or something." Shep was eating the breakfast that was put in front of him when he said that. Harris was staring at him. "What did I say wrong?"

"Nothing. But wouldn't he understand that I was not Gilbert Kane's daughter?" Shep told her that he doubted that Maron could tell him the butler's name, much less anything about his family. "That cold, you think?"

"You probably know everything about the people that work for you. I'd say even though I know you did a background check on all of them, you would still make it a point to know about them. I bet your parents were the same way." Grace assured them that they were. "See? That is not the norm, I don't think, for having a staff. Mostly, from my experience, they're as far from caring shit about the house staff as they are the people that work on the grounds. You care, and that shows that you're someone very special in that regard."

"I'd have to be a niece to him. I know that Gilbert Kane was an elderly man. He had no children, as he worked for that particular house for a great many years. He stayed on when Maron the Moron bought it. A great many of the staff have been leaving over the last months, mostly due to having other jobs. A few have stolen a great deal from the man and disappeared. I would like to find them before this is done too. I have a feeling that they're not far—Maron is a lazy fuck— but I don't know at the present." Shep told her that she could smell the dead now, being a cat. "Seriously?"

"Yes. You have a heightened sense of smell and hearing now. The latter I'm sure you've figured out. But you can smell people too, and remember their scent. That's why when we want to find someone later, we try hard to touch them, or in your case, lick them. All my brothers, if you have noticed, have kissed your hand at some point. So that in the event they have to find you, they can." She asked if she should return the favor. "I would if I were you. You'd be good at finding them now. Much better now that you're a cat."

Harris had a great deal to learn about being a cat. But right now, he just gave her the basics. Mostly things like he'd already told her. She would heal a great deal faster than she could before. She'd live longer. Smelling things and being able to hear well. He also told her that she could, if she wished, be able to shift a part of her body and leave the rest human. Say if she was a cat, she could shift her hand to human to open a door or something.

"I can see that coming in handy." Shep told her that she'd also be able to do all the things like smell and hear even better as a cat. "Okay, so if I were to shift into a cat to find someone, I'd have an easier time than as a person? Cool beans."

He'd never heard her say that before, and laughed hard. Shep loved this woman, and he knew that she was going to keep him on his toes for a very long time. He was really

155

looking forward to growing old with her. When she asked him about children, he had to think on it. Grace told her what she needed to know.

"You'll have children, just like you did. Because you're only what is considered a half breed, any children you have will have to wait until they're twelve or so to see if they shift. However, honey, I've known you all your life, and you never follow rules like most people do." They both laughed. "Also, I want you to eat more meat. It doesn't have to be red, though that would be better for you, but you're a carnivore and they like meat. Feed your cat and she'll be nicer to you when you need her. Not that she can hurt you, but she'll be quicker to help you if she knows that you're not going to take what she needs away."

"I'm going to have a lot to learn about being a cat." She put her hand over his when he told her again that he was sorry. "Don't be. With all this shit going on, it might just save my life. Oh, before I forget to tell you, I quit my job. After this is done with the president, I'm stepping down."

"Woo hoo! Best news that I've heard all year. I'll have you at home all the time." She said for him not to get used to it. She did want to work. "I want you to as well. But less dangerous pursuits, right?"

"Yes. Though I don't know if you're going to be any happier about it. I'm thinking, with my degree, that I should apply for the job as police chief." He said he could live with that a great deal more than hit man. "I hope you're right."

~*~

Sheppard was so happy that he could hardly contain himself. The kids were having such a good time that he was sure that he'd be a great granddaddy soon. He did a little jig as he was walking down the sidewalk toward the grocery store.

He'd been stopping by once a day to see if they had some work that he could do. Sheppard didn't mind sitting around for a little bit, but all the time was making him a little antsy. He needed something to occupy his mind and body, or he was going to be old and stiff before his time. Then yesterday, they'd called and told him he could be the bag boy, if he could keep up.

"If I can keep up. Who do they think they're dealing with?" Laughing a little, he saw his son just as he was moving across the street to the store. "What do you want, James? I don't have time for your foolishness today."

"Why do you hate me so much?" Sheppard said he didn't hate him; he was just disappointed in him. "Why? What is it I ever did to you?"

"You don't have a job. No home that you can call your own. You have six boys that you've not had a thing to do with in more years than I can count." He pretended to be thinking on it. "Oh, and you beat your wife to near death on several occasions. Why did you do that to them, James? She was a wonderful woman. And those boys are about the best there is. Did you hear that Shep is married now? Got himself a good woman to love."

"Why would that make any difference to me? I met her. She's a ball buster, and the wrong type of woman for my son." He asked him what she'd said to him. "You heard her, Dad. She threatened me about coming around. Not even the other boys will have a thing to do with me. That's just not right."

"Why? Because they won't give you money? I'm not either. Now get on away from here before I'm late to work."

James asked him why he was working. "I love to work. And talk. I can talk all day if I want to, and if I have me a captive crowd, then I'm in heaven."

"You're expecting me to believe that someone is going to pay you to talk all day?" He said that he was bag boy for the grocery store. "That is a kid's job, not an old man like you are. What if you get hurt? Then what will happen?"

"Will you be concerned if I'm hurt, son?" He didn't answer him, and that was answer enough for Sheppard. "You're such a disappointment, James. More than I realized when you were growing up. Why didn't you try and make it work out between you and Jill Ann? I already told you what a great woman she was."

"To you. You had her eating out of your hand. But for me, all she ever did was bitch and complain all the time. Like I needed to work when there was money in the banks." Sheppard told him that the money was hers. "She was my wife. Why didn't she share it with me?"

"More than likely she didn't think you were up to paying it back. You do know that you have to give as good as you get, don't you? I mean, if you want something, then work for it to get paid. Money just don't grow on trees." James rolled his eyes at him. "I don't have time for your tomfoolery today. Go on back to the rock you were living under and leave me alone."

"I need some money, Dad. I'm your son. Help me out so that I can have a decent meal." He asked him what sort of meal that was to him. "A steak in a fine restaurant. A nice fat potato with all the trimmings. I want to have a slice of pie for dessert. Have a nice glass of wine too. You can spot me that much, can't you? I mean, I've seen the improvements to the house that I used to own. Let me have some money."

"You never own diddly, you fool. All you did was waste money until Jill Ann had to put them boys to work to make up for it all. There wasn't no point in telling you no, either—you just beat them all until you got what you wanted." Sheppard laughed. "I guess you noticed that they're all a bit bigger than you are, so you'll just leave them be. Too bad really—I think they'd all take you on just to have you out of their lives."

"What a thing to say to me. I'm their father, damn it. Just as you are mine. Why don't you just fucking fork over the money and let me be on my way?" Sheppard dug in his pocket for his little wallet. "That's more like it. Thanks, Dad. It's about time you're starting to— What the hell is this? A quarter? What the hell am I supposed to do with a fucking quarter?"

"I'd use it to call someone up that gives two hoots about what you want."

Laughing, he entered the grocery store. After getting his apron on, Sheppard was ready for his first day on the job.

He wasn't worried that James would hurt him. The boy had better know better. Here he was pushing near abouts sixty himself, and he acted like he was ten years old. Moron.

Between customers he had plenty of time to think on things. Mostly it was about his grandsons, but he did have an occasion to think about James. He had been a disappointment since he'd been a teenager. Probably before that. It had occurred to him that his wife had hidden a great deal from him about their only child. And now here he was a grown assed man, and acting like the world owed him something.

"Are you all right, Mr. Marshall? This isn't too much for you, is it?" He told her that he was having the time of his life.

159

"You look like you're thinking hard on something. I saw you talking to your son. Are you worried that he'll go to prison after he's taken to court next week?"

"I didn't know a thing about that, Erin. What did he do that has him that bound up by the law?" She told him that she'd only heard about it yesterday, and told him as much as she knew, which to him was a great deal. "I had no idea that he'd resorted to stealing cars. Was anyone hurt when he wrecked it?"

"Mr. Brown lost his job over it, but they gave it back to him when he told them what had happened. I guess James had been out with some buddies of his, no nicer than he is, and he was showing off. I only know that much because my dad is a cop. He said that he totaled that car so badly that they had to use two wreckers to pull it out of the river, then use the jaws of life to get Mr. Horn out. He died, you know. But they have yet to charge him with that. Daddy doesn't know if they will or not because he wasn't driving. Mr. Horn was driving it when it wrecked. But James, he stole the car. They have him on one of those house recorder things taking it."

He wasn't sure that this little girl should be telling things that her daddy did, but he only thanked her. Sheppard wondered if any of the boys knew about it, and figured that Harris would know before anyone else. She was keeping tabs on James, she'd told him. When there was another break in what he was doing, he reached out to her.

*I knew about it. But since there was little to nothing that we could do about it, I thought it best not to ruin your good mood about it. Grandda, you have to admit, you've been in a really good mood for some time now.* He said that he had been, and wasn't upset that she didn't tell him. *He's going to be jailed for grand theft, as well as other things. He was seen driving the car away, and since he doesn't have a license anymore, they got him on that too.* Sheppard asked her why he was out and about. *There were four men that night, two we know of and two we don't. For some reason, the police have it in their head that he was paid to steal the car. Which means to them that one of the other two are responsible too. I think they should get rid of all their asses, but that's just me.*

*I just saw James. He was begging me for enough money to go out and buy himself a nice steak dinner. On me.* She said that sounded like him. *I have a girl here that I'm working with. I don't want her to get into trouble, but she was telling me all about what happened at the police station that her daddy is a cop with. She even told me details that I'm sure the public shouldn't be knowing. Like Mr. Horn was driving when the car was found in the river.*

*I'll have a talk with him about it. I've decided to take over the running of the department. There are too many things that are going left unsolved. Not that they're a bad lot, they're just a lazy bunch. And if they're sharing information with their kids, who in turn tells the county, it's small wonder that they can catch anyone. Just knowing that the police are after you would make someone run, don't you think?* Sheppard agreed with her on that. *I'll keep you informed if you want. Don't talk to him about it unless he talks first. But, like most of the town, he probably figures that he's free and clear since most crimes don't get solved or taken care of.*

*I can see that too, my dear. I'll just let Erin tell me all about it, and see where it goes here too.* He laughed. *She might give me more than you have. She seems to be well informed for a cashier.*

Sheppard really was having a good time. The people that came in, they all remembered him from when his wife would shop there. A lot of them told him that they'd thought it was wonderful that he'd push the cart for her and load them on the belt to be run out. They asked if he'd put the groceries away when they got home.

"She'd not let me do that. I put them in the wrong places, she told me." He laughed, thinking about her fussing at him about where he put things. "My missus would get a little mad when she'd find things that should have been in the cabinet in the refrigerator, or things in that contraption in the freezer part."

The rest of his shift was easy for him. He was on his feet a good deal more than he was used to, but he walked a great deal, so it wasn't as bad as it could have been for him. Walking home, he saw people that he'd just worked with having a cookout or such.

They were having steaks tonight. Grace had come over and asked him what he wanted with his. All he could think about was apple pie. She said that she could surely have him one of those made. He knew that she could. It was one of the best things that came out of that kitchen so far as he was concerned. Sheppard surely did love living with Shep and Harris. They knew how to treat an old man.

He was nearly home when he saw his son again. Thankfully he'd not seen him yet, so Sheppard stepped around the corner and watched him talking to another man. Sheppard didn't know who he was, this other man, but he was large, like fat large, and he drove a silver Porsche. It would be easy to trace, he figured, since there wasn't that many people that could afford them anymore. And this one looked to be in perfect shape.

After the big man hit James, he got into his car and drove away. Good thing that James was fast on his feet, or he might have gotten run over. Taking a picture of the license plate number, Sheppard went on home. He'd give it to Harris. She'd be able to do a great deal with it, he thought.

The more he thought about it, the more he didn't care. If James got himself mixed up with other people then he would have to deal with it. Besides, Sheppard knew that his Harris would take care of the shit. Smiling about it, he deleted the picture and walked home.

# Chapter 12

Shep followed Harris through Benson's house. He was his cat in the event that she might need him to make Benson piss himself. It was fine by him—he could be with her and try and keep her safe.

Benson hadn't been heard from in a couple of days, and Howard had wanted her to check on him. Harris knew that he had killed himself—or worse yet, had been killed by Maron before he'd been arrested. The meeting with Maron still bothered Shep a little, but Harris said that it was no less than she had expected.

"Who the hell are you?" Maron had been pissy as soon as they walked up to his cell. Being that he was on the government payroll, he was in a federal prison, which sounded much better than it really was. He had a guard at his door at all times, military that couldn't be bought, as Maron told them. As well as very little time out of doors for him. That was another point that he made to Harris, AKA, Danielle Kane, the butler's niece.

"You killed my uncle, Gilbert Kane." He asked her who that was. "My uncle was your butler. Didn't you even try to learn his name before you shot him?"

"It was an accident. Just as I've been telling these people here. I was dealing with a bitch and he came in the room just as I ran her off." Sure he had, Shep thought. "When he opened the door, I thought it was her and fired at him. I didn't mean to, but apparently that doesn't mean anything to these people."

Maron went on and on about how he'd made a mistake, one that anyone would, and Harris kept getting more and more mouthy with him. She was never mad, but she wanted him to be pissed off enough to say something. He never did, as a matter of fact, but Harris sure had enjoyed herself. He had too, and still laughed about it.

Now she was checking on the other man who had been a part of this shit. The house was deadly quiet, but neither of them made a sound. Just as it looked like no one was home, Benson came out of the basement with too large sacks in his hands.

"Hello, Benson. Are you going someplace?" Harris didn't look like she was anything but a well formed woman. Her hair was covered, face and hands too. The only thing that he'd been able to see of her was her eyes. And those did not look happy to be here. "I asked you a question, dumb shit. Where are you going?"

"Who the fuck are you? And how did you get into my home? I'm calling the police." Harris pointed to the cell that was laying on the counter by him. "Get out of here. I didn't allow you in, and I want you out of my house."

"You see, that's not going to work for me." She put down

her hand, and Shep moved to stand beside her. It had the desired effect in that Benson screamed. "This is why that doesn't work for me. You see, you've been up to no good, Benson. As of this morning, we have stopped your caravan of trucks coming into and out of the States, and you'd not believe the shit that we found on the fuckers. Were you about to start a war? Looks like it to me."

"You have no right to do that. Who are you?" She didn't answer Benson. Shep really hadn't expected her to. "I'll give you one of these bags of money if you just go away and never say a word. You'd like that, wouldn't you? I mean, it's a lot of money."

"I have enough, thanks." He told her that no one could never have enough money. "Only bad guys think that. Where did all this come from? You haven't sold off the guns you have yet, so that can't be it. Drugs? Well, those have been stopped too, haven't they?"

"Did you stop them? Do you have any idea how much trouble you've gotten me into? Christ, I have buyers all over the country wondering where their shit is. Davidson told me to send it off as soon as I was informed that it was here. Now, listen here. You just leave now after telling me where my things are." She only sat down at the table and Shep laid at her feet. "How the hell does someone get a jaguar that big to do what they want it to do? That must have cost you a fortune. How about I buy him off you? Any price, you name it."

"He'd only eat you alive, and that wouldn't be any fun for me, now would it?" She petted him on the head and he purred. "You work for someone. If you'd just played along like I wanted, then I'd have him too. But you had to go and do the silent thing, and so I had to come and see what you're about. I don't think anyone thought that you'd be alive. I hoped you would be so that I can hurt you, but you were leaving town without saying goodbye to me. How mean is that, Benson?"

"You're not going to hurt me. I'm the vice president of the United States." Harris told him that he *was* the VP, past tense. "No, I'm him. You can ask Howard about it. He'll tell you."

"You see, everyone thinks that you're dead. That you killed yourself. I can't let an opportunity like that go. It's the perfect thing for me to use, don't you agree?" His face paled and he dropped both bags. "Are you getting it now? Do you know who I am?"

"Cora Banks. The government hit man." She nodded and told him that he got extra points for knowing her. "You're here to kill me. Who hired you?"

"Who do you think hired me? You do know that I'm freelance now. Now that you've tried to have me killed. Also, I think you know who hired me, don't you?" He nodded, and this was what they'd been waiting on. Someone to come clean with who they worked for. Harris stood up and took out her gun. "He did say that I could have fun with you before you ended up on the wrong end of a rope. I think suicide by hanging is so overrated. I was thinking more along the lines of putting you into a tub of warm water and slicing open your wrists. The water will start out pink. Then after a short time, it'll get darker. After —"

"You have to let me go. I'll do whatever you want, just don't kill me." She said that her contact was promising her a million dollars for making him look good. "I'll give you four. I have it right here. Take one of these bags, and that'll be four million. That should be enough."

"I don't know. It sounds good, but what if he doesn't use me again for a job? What will I live on?" He told her that she could kill Mr. Tanager and that she could have all his money. "You think that would be all it takes? What about my travel time?"

"He just lives in Columbus, Ohio. I don't think it'll be that much of a hardship for you where you live. Just go there, kill him, and you can live in his big mansion on Twenty-Fourth Street." He grinned like the deal was a done one. "It's really nice. I've been in it before when I was in the area. Not as nice as the one I have in DC, but it's nice. He hasn't any family, he told me once, and spends all his money on whatever he wants."

"Tanager on Twenty-Fourth Street—have you got it?" Benson looked around and asked her who she was talking to. "The people that work for me and Howard. You might remember him—he's president of the United States. Which I believe trumps your VP status. By a great deal, I think."

The army guards came in just as she was stretching her arms above her head. Shep kept an eye on the man—he was much too casual about what was going on. And when he pulled his gun, Shep was ready to leap at him when shots were fired. They weren't from Harris, he knew that. She had thrown her body over him to protect him, he thought.

Harris had been told not to fire unless he fired first. The two men that had their rifles out and aimed at Benson were not moving, but they had both fired at the same time, blowing Benson's head off, and his bags had dumped all over the kitchen.

The clean-up was long and drawn out. They were marking

things which were put into a catalog of events, and things were being recorded too. It wasn't until he'd been allowed to shift and to dress that he realized what they were doing. Searching the entire house. And they were not being very neat about it either. Sofas were cut into. Walls were marked with cans of spray. He had to ask one of the people searching why they were doing that.

"It means that we've checked the wall for safes. Most of the time it's not as easy as moving a picture and there it is. Sometimes they are buried in the wall with plaster over them so that when they leave in a hurry, they just knock out a wall." Shep thanked him. "You're a cat, correct?"

"Yes, do you need me for something?" The man, the one that he thought only reported to Harris, said he needed someone to sniff out the basement. They were looking for bodies. "My wife, she's looking outside, isn't she?"

"Yes, but to be honest, Mr. Marshall, I'd like to get out of this place. It's giving me the creeps. This guy had a great job, and he fucked it all up for the love of one thing. Power." He asked him about money. "Money usually comes with power, but you have to have the power first. It smells of treason around here."

"I'll help."

He made his way to the basement, where two men were searching the walls. After they turned their backs, Shep stripped down, this time taking off his clothing. He didn't have any more with him. The smell took his breath away, and he wondered how he could tell them what he was finding.

"Mr. Marshall, my name is Peter. I'm a human, but I'm all right with communicating with you. I spoke to your wife earlier, and she was all right with it too." Nodding, he took the man's hand into his mouth and bit down. It wasn't that much, but he could now communicate with him. "What is it you smell?"

*Lye. A great deal of it too.* Peter asked him where he smelled it coming from. Instead of trying to tell him, Shep led him over to the furthest wall and pawed at it. *Not on the floor, but behind the wall here. Could that be possible?*

"I don't know why not. It's no crazier than anything else that we're discovering in this house." After calling down several men, the wall was taken down. Not only was there a room behind the wall, but there was a pallet full of lye wrapped up and ready to go. It was the bodies that they were most concerned with. "There are seven in here that we can count. He has them stacked up on top of each other like logs for sale."

He moved out of the way and watched the men work. None of them commented on the fact that a large spotted jaguar was in the room with them, nor did they seem frightened of him. When the last body was pulled out, he was asked to go in and sniff around again.

There was another room behind the one they'd just torn out. It wasn't lye this time, nor bodies, but something more. It was filled with blueprints for every building and home in the area. They also found a way out of that area into the yard above. They had planned this to the tee.

"Do you smell who might have been down here with Benson?" He told him that Davidson had been down here a great deal. But no one else. Harris was asked to come and see if she could smell anything else, and she said that she couldn't. Now they were headed to the house back in Ohio, not too far from where she and Shep lived. Tanager was next on their list

171

of people whose home they needed to search.

~*~

"Why would they need the plans to all the houses in the area, do you think?" Harris didn't answer Shep. She had a feeling that she was right in her assumptions, and didn't want to say in case she was wrong about it. *Do you know or do you not know? I have a feeling you know.*

She looked at him. The fact that he'd said that through their link made her realize just how much he knew her. Nodding at him, he nodded back and said no more. They were headed back to Ohio to the other home, and she was sure that things were about to go to shit.

After a short flight by private jet, they reached Columbus and picked up their car. Within minutes they had reached their destination.

The house was nondescript. Trees in the front yard shaded the driveway, just like every other house on the block. There was a wooden fence in the back yard to keep the neighbors from snooping around. No toys in the yard. There weren't any flowers either. Just a house on a street like any other.

The first thing that hit her when she walked in was the scent. Harris knew that she'd not have been able to smell that if she hadn't been a cat. It was, being a cat, affording her all kinds of perks that she didn't have before. Watching Shep when he entered, his face paled and he looked at her. Yes, she thought, he knows too.

The house was devoid of furniture other than in the living room. There was a fridge, but it was empty. A larger room held a single cot, but nothing more. There were no dressers, no computers. Nor were they going to find a safe or anything else that would attach this house to the person that had had contact with Maron and Benson.

Confused, the rest of the men with them searched every part of the house and garage attached to it until they had exhausted themselves. It was a dead end, they said. Not even the bathroom had been used, it looked like. No towels, shower curtain, or toilet paper. Like the person living here, it was a front. And Harris knew all about fronts.

They set two people to watch the place. The rest left. Harris and Shep were thanked for their help, and were told they'd call them when they had more information. After they left, pulling around the corner to wait, her and Shep moved back to the house and climbed into the basement door that Shep had managed to unlock from the inside.

The door was just where she'd thought it would be. It wasn't as well hidden as the ones at the other home, but she knew what to look for now. Stepping into the darkness, she stood there with Shep as she tried to think what she needed to do now.

"I'll walk this, you go and confront him. If anyone tries to escape through this way, I'll be in the tunnel waiting for them." She asked if he'd be his cat. "I will if it makes you feel any better."

"It would. Just because I know that you're much stronger as a cat, and you can heal faster if you shift. I don't know what to do about your clothing. But I would feel better if you were your jaguar." He said that he'd be all right until she came to get him. "I love you, Shep. You know who this is, don't you? Will it bother you if you have to take him down? I mean, because of who he is?"

"No." The word was said with so much finality that she believed him. "You go now, and I'll start walking. It won't take me too long, I don't think. My cat could use a good run anyway. When we're done here, we'll both go on a run and see what sort of trouble we can get into."

Kissing him goodbye, Harris slipped out of the basement again and walked to the car. She was going to have to talk to someone about having the men here retrained or fired. Her and Shep had just spent an hour in the house, and no one had been the wiser. Fuckers.

Getting to where she was going might be a tad tricky. She wondered if she should warn people about this, but Harris could only think of one person that needed to know. Reaching out to Sheppard, she told him what her and Shep had discovered and said that she was sorry.

*Don't be. Bound to be happening sometime. You want me to ride with you? Honestly, honey, I'm in Columbus now with Oakley. We was doing some shopping for the party to mark the end of summer.* Harris told him that she'd like that, please. *You tell us where you are and we'll meet you there. Oakley, he's going to want to come too, you know. Just because we know him.*

*Yes, that'll be fine. So long as he knows that I'm in charge of this. No heroics please. I have enough going on right now.* Sheppard laughed and said that they'd be good. *Thank you for coming with me. You guys will be a nice distraction on the trip.*

The drive was sort of boring. Harris didn't talk to the other two much, but knowing that they were there was very helpful to her. Who to talk to, that was the question. Who did she tell so that things would not hit the fan when she confronted him?

Harris still didn't have a clue when they arrived at the house the next morning. She was exhausted, but exhilarated too. It would be done today, and after that, she'd have to figure out what to do with the information that she had.

She knew this house like she did her own. No one there tried to stop her, nor did they ask her what she was doing there so early in the morning. Harris spoke to a couple of people on her way in, and took the stairs up two at a time to the apartment there. As soon as she opened the door, everything about this fell into place.

"Hello, Harris. Did we have an appointment? I'm sort of running behind today a little. Oh, did you find Benson yet? I'm sure that he's going to run, don't you think?" She told Howard that he was dead. "Dead? No, I don't think so. Did you kill the VP, Harris?"

"No, you did, Howard, when you got them to try and move you out of the office. It would have created a huge surge in your popularity, wouldn't it? To have been nearly killed off by your own VP? What happened to you?" Howard sat down and said nothing. "You might be interested to know that Maron is in jail too. They're searching his house as we speak. What do you think they'll find there?"

"Nothing. At least with my name on it. They only knew me as Tanager. How the fuck did you figure it out? Not that you're going to live long enough to be able to tell anyone. I've had all the cameras in here turned off." She didn't comment. Along with her ability to turn them off, Harris could turn them on at will too. Hopefully Oakley was doing what she'd asked of him in the computer rooms. Harris reached out to Allison and told her to get Lily out of the building and someplace safe. "They were going to kill Lily for me. Did you know that? I'll have to do it now. Not that it bothers me overly much. She's been a drag for a very long time. The sympathy vote will put me over the top too, don't you think?"

Oakley said it was a go, and Harris could have wept with

joy.

"What I think is that you're a sick fuck. How did you figure me into all this? I'm sure that you had good reason to lead me along like a sad pup." Howard told her she had been doing fine until now. "Well, I'm sorry to have burst your plans, fuck head. You're going to prison right along with Maron. Unless I have to kill you first."

"You won't. I know you too well in that. You're not very smart, not nearly as smart as you think you are." She didn't say anything as Allison was telling her that Lily and her were in the safe room. That she couldn't find Toby. "Cat got your tongue, Harris?"

"You have no idea. Where is Toby? It must have cramped your style to have him hanging around you all the time." He told her that after they got back, he'd simply killed him. "I see. That must have been difficult for you. Toby isn't a push over."

"You're right about that. I did try and kill him by beating him to death, but that proved to be more hurtful to me than to him, I think. Then while he was recuperating in the hospital, it was nothing for me to slip in there and give him poison. It worked wonders." Toby wasn't dead then. Unless Howard gave him way more than he was used to taking of every poison on the market, he would have been able to stand it. "You look happy. What is it? Are you happy that young Toby is dead? After I take care of you, breaking and entering in the White House should turn a lot of heads. Then added to the attempted murder of myself, I'll find my wife and kill her off too. You will be thought of as the one that killed her. Just so you know."

"You have a plan for everything, don't you, Howard?

Not that it's going to matter, I guess. Not when everything that you're saying to me is being broadcast to the world. You might say that I'm a great deal smarter than you have given me credit for." He said that he didn't believe her. "You don't? Well, how sad for you. Go ahead, turn on the television and see for yourself. I've not seen it myself yet, but you go ahead, and we'll watch it together."

"You lie." She said that she rarely did unless it suited her, but this was the truth. "You have nothing, and now you're trying to trick me into doing something that has me turning my back on you. Well, it won't happen, Harris. As far as I'm concerned, you're as good as dead now." He pulled out the gun and pointed it at her.

"You really think that is going to give you what you want, Howard? No one is going to believe you after this. You won't be getting the sympathy vote as you wanted. Nor will anyone give a shit that you've plotted to have your lovely wife killed. Which you won't be able to, by the way. She's in the safe room with Allison." He laughed, and she just smiled at him. "You think I'm funny?"

"I do. You're grasping at straws, Harris. I have this all in the bag. And thanks to you, Benson is dead. Maron, who never met me, is going to prison. They were stupid anyway, if they thought that this was going to work out for them. The people are going to be so happy that I made it through all this without a single scratch that they'll beg me to be president for life. And you know what? I think I'd like setting myself up as dictator."

"Dictator, huh? Well, good luck with that. Perhaps you can practice on your inmates. If you live that long." Howard stood up and put the gun to her chest. "Won't work, you know.

There are enough cameras on you right now that you're going to be caught before you can pull the trigger."

"You think so?" The door behind her burst open and four men came in, pointing guns in their direction. Howard smiled at her as he spoke to the men. "This woman here tried to kill me and my wife. I want her put into shackles right away."

"Sir, put the gun down." Howard told them again what she'd done to him. Or the lie that he'd been working on. "Sir, if you don't put the gun down, I'm going to have to fire. Now, do as you are told and drop the gun."

"Do you have any idea who I am? I'm the fucking president of the United States. I want you to arrest this woman right now."

He was thrown to the ground and the gun went off. No one moved as they tried to figure out what had happened.

# Chapter 13

After finishing at the house, Shep followed Harris to the White House, and ended up in an area right outside the White House as his cat. He knew that something was going on—there were news crews all over the place. Staying back in the trees that were close enough that he could see and not be seen, he was startled when his grandda brought him something to put on.

"Now, I don't want you to freak out. All right?" He stopped in pulling his pants over his leg. "Shep, I can feel your tension right now. Didn't I tell you not to freak out? Harris is hurt, but she's going to be just fine."

"What happened?" Grandda asked him if he'd heard that she was all right. "I heard you. Did you hear me ask you want happened?"

"That president, or that ex-president, he shot her. In the arm, but she's just fine. Pissy about it—her words, not mine." Grandda told him that she was at the hospital, and that she'd sent him to find him. "I've been all over this place looking for you. I should have called out, but I was fearful that you'd feel my tension too."

"I want to see her." He said that they would, but they had to rescue Oakley first. "What happened to him? And on that note, why are you here?"

"She wanted some company, and I was with your brother. We rode along and kept her company. When we got here, she asked Oakley what he knew about computers, and he said plenty. Did you know that?" Shep growled at his grandda. "I'm working up to it. Anyway, he fixed the computers so that it would broadcast what was going on in that room up there all over the networks. Did the trick too, I'm thinking. Howard is in a military prison, screaming about how my Harris framed him. When all along, everybody that had a television was watching it."

They were walking to the car when he thought of Lily. "She's all right, isn't she? I know that Harris sent those people in to help with guarding them. Oh Christ, Grandda, that man, Toby, he was on the president all that time. Did he kill him?"

Grandda said that he'd tried. "Harris trained people on poisons too. Told them how to take a little each day or week until they could build up a tolerance to it. He ended up disappearing from the first hospital, and ended up in the hospital that Harris is in. She's all right—I told you that, didn't I?" Grandda was looking like he was going to cry, so Shep stopped walking and hugged him. "I surely don't want anything to happen to her, Shep. She's brought me back from playing dead. Threatened me like I was no more than a child, but it got me moving. I'd not be here without her doing that."

"Grandda, I love you. But if you don't let me go and see my wife, I'm going to hurt someone. Not you, because I love you, but someone is going to get hurt." After another quick hug, they got into the car and made their way to the hospital. "How do I get to see her? And what do I need to do to help out Oakley? Is he all right?"

"Yes, he's really fine. I think he's overwhelmed with all the newspaper people wanting to know how he did that. I tell you, I thought he was going to have a kitten when they shoved the microphones in his face." Shep asked if he needed them. "No, I was just joking with you. I guess I'm not good at jokes much."

There were as many television crews there as there had been at the White House. A man in a marine uniform came out to get them as soon as Grandda made a quick call. They were escorted in, with a group of all the branches of the service around them. People wanted to know how they were related to their hero. The two of them and the man who had come to get them got in one of the elevators, and they rode it all the way to the top floor.

"She's a hero to me too." Shep told Grandda that she was a hero to him too. Harris had saved him as much as she'd saved Grandda. "She's going to be fit to be tied—you know that, don't you? I bet she fusses at you the most."

"I'm not going to give her any chance to do that. I'm going to take her into my arms and kiss her senseless." Then he was going to beat her ass for getting hurt, but he didn't think that telling Grandda that would get him any points. "I love that woman so much."

"She did her country proud, Mr. Marshall. Your wife, I've never met her, but I've heard that if you want it done right, you should call on her. She's my hero too." The marine smiled as he continued. "You give her a kiss for me too, sir.

181

She might be quiet long enough then so that you can get a word in edgewise."

As soon as he was let into her room—the guard had to check him for weapons—he did just what he had said he was going to do. Shep pulled her from the bed and held her to him, kissing her hard enough that she had to know how glad he was to have her around. When he laid her back on the bed, he held her hand and sat down. Neither of them spoke as Grandda told them what was going on.

The television was on mute in her room, but he could see the pres—Howard talking to Harris. While he didn't know what was being said, Shep could see the gun that he had on her. Kissing the back of her hand, Shep finally was able to talk to her.

"I love you." She cried then, and told him how much she loved him. "Then why are you upset? Are you hurt more than they said you were? I'm going to roll some heads if they're letting you suffer needlessly."

"I'm fine. I promise you. But Howard was willing to kill Lily. Just for a bigger vote, Shep." He told her that he was glad that they were all safe. "Howard thought that Toby was dead. He was talking with the Feds before I had your brother broadcast things to everyone. I felt that since they put him there in office, they needed to see what sort of person he really was."

"Have I told you how incredibly smart you are? You are. Brilliant." He kissed her again, just happy that he could hold her hand while the nurse fussed about Harris not lying still. She blamed it on him. "I had to hold her. I'm so sorry."

"It's all right, Mr. Marshall. I can understand that. There I was watching the monitors, and it popped up on my feed.

I was so surprised it took me several minutes to realize that it was live, and that that mad man was trying to hurt this woman here. And he wanted to kill his own lovely wife. Why, I tell you, had I been in that room with him, I'd have just smacked the shit right out of him. Pardon my cursing, but he just made me so mad. Then he was screaming that he was president and all."

After she left, the three of them started laughing. She was full of spit, Grandda said, and they both agreed. Shep asked Harris when she was going to get to go home. Soon, he hoped.

"They said that I'd be better off staying here for a couple of days. Just until the press let some of this go. I don't think they will. They're a tenacious group." He pouted and she laughed. "They're giving me a private room with the guards at the door until I'm ready to leave. Also, and you'll love this, I'm to have my husband in here with me. They'll bring you in a bed later today."

"Well that will be a waste. I'm not sleeping without you." Grandda stood up and said that he was going home. "Don't go yet, Grandda. You helped me out, and I can't thank you enough."

"You and Harris, you enjoy your stay here. I'll let the staff know that you're going to be here for a while. They probably seen it on television too." Grandda said that he was tired anyway.

"I thank you so much for helping her out. You need anything, you just tell us. All right?"

"A great grandbaby would be wonderful. I know how things work, and she's not in heat or whatever humans call it, but you give me that and I'll be the happiest man on this here earth." Harris told him that they wanted that too. "Well then,

183

I couldn't be happier. Until I'm holding a baby."

Grandda was still laughing as he made his way out of the room. Shep got into the small bed with Harris and held her. To him, there was nothing better than having her in his arms. When she seemed to have fallen asleep, he knew that she'd not been sleeping well. Shep thought of all the days he was going to have with this woman.

There were times when he caught himself thinking that this couldn't be true, that she wasn't his wife and that they didn't live in a huge house. He had money, but it didn't compare to what she had. But Harris told him that it didn't matter whose money it was, so long as they were happy at the end of the day. He liked that about her.

Shep must have dozed off, because someone knocking at the door startled him awake. He'd not realized that Harris was still armed, so when she pulled out her gun and aimed it at the door, he just waited to see what the fuck was going on.

"Major General Marshall, the FBI would like to speak to you." She asked the voice what they wanted. "They said they wanted to debrief you on what happened today."

"They are well aware that I was there, aren't they?" He said that they were and the handle on the door turned. "Someone comes in that door without me saying it's all right, I'm going to blow their fucking head off. Who is it, and do they have identification?"

The laughter on the other side of the door had her smiling. Either she knew who it was or she was happy to be able to blow their heads off. When the door opened and a very large man was standing there, he looked at the two of them and laughed harder.

"Well, well, well. If it's not Cora Banks all banged up.

Or do you go by your given name now. Harrison Elizabeth Parker?" She told him that she was married, and what her name was now. "Good for you. This man, does he know what a fucking pain in the arse you are? I'd be happy to tell him if he doesn't."

"Shep, I'd like for you to meet Jamison Luster. He's the head of the FBI agency. When he decides to show up for work, that is." Jamison said that she wounded him. "I doubt that's true. As far as I know, you've never had a heart."

Shep got out of the bed, embarrassed to be caught there for some reason.

Jamison and Harris hugged and Shep got his hand nearly ripped off by the other man. Jamison sat down in the chair that Shep had been in earlier. Shep was sure that he heard the chair groan when Jamison adjusted his weight around. He was a very large man.

"I've come by to see if I can convince you to come work for— Don't shake your head no when you have no idea what it is I want from you. You'd be good at it, too." Harris told him no, she wasn't working like that anymore. "You still don't know what I'm talking about."

"It doesn't matter. I'm done getting shot at, stabbed, and nearly poisoned. I'm tired of working. I want to stay at home and become a lady of leisure." Jamison laughed. "You don't think I can do it? I want to have children. Children to whom I don't want to have to explain why I come home with bullet holes all over my body. Don't you think I've given enough to my country?"

"You've given more in this one day than a great many people do in a lifetime. Including me." Harris thanked him. "I want you to consider what I'm asking you, Harris. It won't put you out in the way of gunfire. You won't have to worry about money, and I promise you that you'll never have to leave the comforts of your home if you let me do a little tweaking to what you've no doubt already put into your house."

"I can be at the comfort of my home without you tweaking anything there. As far as money is concerned, I don't have to worry about that either. Even if I never have another check come in, it's more than enough for me to live off of with my family." He asked again if she'd just let him explain. "It doesn't matter. Say it or not, the answer is still no."

"I want you to take over my job." She asked him what he'd said. Shep could smell it then. The man was dying. "I'm not long for this world. I have about six months, they said, but even coming here has done me in. I have cancer all over my body, and there is squat that they can do about it."

"I'm sorry."

Jamison waved her off. "It'll be a good job for you. You can train them to be like that group that you hired for yourself. That Toby, I spoke to him and his sister, and they had nothing but wonderful things to say about you. The only reason that that boy is still here is because you taught him something that I never would have to my men. Some of the things they've been taking to build up their bodies is toxic. But you saved his life."

"He saved me on enough occasions." Jamison said he knew that too. "I'm sorry that you're ill. I truly am. But I don't want to work. Not ever again. I don't like people."

Jamison stood up and tossed a packet on her table that was just out of Harris's reach. She asked him what it was, and the big man laughed again. When Harris got up to have a look at it, Jamison took it from her and kissed her on the cheek.

186

"I have always loved you like you were my own daughter, Harris. I'm glad in a way that you never told me about what was going on. You know as well as I that I would never have let you go in and do what you did without getting approval, as well as taking more men than you needed." He laughed a little bit. "You did this on your own, on your own terms. There isn't a better person in the world for taking my job than you. Nice to meet you, Sheppard. You're a good man too."

When he left them, Harris took the envelope off the table again from where Jamison had put it the second time. When she opened it, Harris strung together a string of curse words that made him blush. Then she looked at him, and he could see fire in her eyes. Even his cat seemed to have backed away from her.

"Its my identification badge and a list of perks that I get as new head of the department of the Feds. The mother fucker didn't come here to ask me to take the job. I already had it. I'm going to.... Does anyone do anything on the up and up anymore?"

Shep couldn't help it, he started laughing. Even when Harris threw her pillow and slippers at him, he laughed all the harder. Harris was in charge of the FBI, and he couldn't have been happier.

~*~

Harris wasn't pissed any longer, but she still wasn't happy with Jamison. The man had been slick, she'd give him that. But she still wasn't going to take the job. No way.

"I guess you've been thinking about the job." Harris smiled at Grandda. "You should take it, honey. As he said, there isn't a person around that could do a better job than you can."

187

"He said that my offices would be fixed here. It's been started on with the barn that was back there. What if I had wanted horses?" Sheppard told her that they couldn't have horses around them. "Because of us being cats."

"Yes. If we had a couple of foals around us from the day they were born, then maybe we could train them to be around us, but not an older horse. Cows and other domestic animals are like that too. Cats, though, the kitten variety, as you can imagine, they have no such troubles with us." She didn't ask him if he was serious. It had occurred to her that while he was the best man she'd known, he rarely got sarcasm, nor did he get that many jokes. "I was going to ask you something. It's not that important, not really, but I do have a need for the answer. How soon did you know that it was Howard that was doing all that? I've spoken to Lily too. She's been cleared of all things that went on."

"I know about Lily. She's been moved out of the White House, at her request, and put in a location where people aren't going to be able to find her. I'm glad, however, that she's talking to you. I did worry about her." He said that he was using the phone that she'd given him. "Good. As for Howard. I didn't know until we were at Benson's house. I wasn't sure until we entered the house in Columbus. I could smell him there."

"I hadn't any idea until I saw it on the news feed. Oakley is being hounded by the press about his help on this too. I'm glad that you fixed it up so that he was left alone for a little while. Now that you're home, honey, hopefully things will calm down for a bit." She told him not to count on it. "No, I really wasn't."

"Shep has decided to go back to college and get his

doctorate in mechanical engineering. He said that he learned a great deal out on that rigger, but he thinks he might have been better at his job, at least smarter than his boss, if he could have more of an understanding. He might even come up with a better way of drilling out there that doesn't have so much waste in the water." Sheppard said that he was proud of him. "Yes, I am as well. He's a good man."

Harris had been home for a week now, and the phone was ringing off the hook. Two of the calls had been from news stations from around the world. She'd be happy when things were settled, though she didn't hold out much hope of that happening soon.

"By the way, I've talked to the boys, and they're ready to have a meeting with their dad. I don't know what will come of it—he's not the sharpest tool in the case—but he might be reasoned with." She told him that she was supposed to be there so that she would convince him that things were the way they were for him. "Yes, well, that's going to go over as well as him thinking that he's going to win the lotto or something. The man might be my son, but he's dumber than a bag of rocks. For all I know, the rocks could be smarter than him."

"You still love him, don't you, Grandda? I mean, he is stupid, but you love him. Right?" Sheppard told her that he would always love him, but he didn't have to like him. Nor respect him. "I don't think any of them respect him anymore. He's coming over Sunday to have dinner with us all. I doubt very much if he'll show without his hands being out for more, but I told them I'd behave."

Sheppard laughed. "You are a good girl, Harris. A good girl." He looked over the package that she had been going through when he came into the room. "That looks like a lot of fancy stuff you got there. Is there anything that you really want?"

"Not really. But I'm not taking the job." He asked her why not. "I want to have a family. Sit in front of the television if I have a mind to, and enjoy that with my husband. What happens when I have children? Am I supposed to cart them to the White House for briefings?"

"Who have they got in that spot, now that you mention it?" She told him what she knew. "Speaker of the House. Well, I'm assuming that he's checked out with all this other stuff. As a country, I don't think that we need any more crap going on."

"No, we do not." She moved to the table and left the box there. It was a bunch of books on the new equipment that was being installed in the barn. "Now, I have a question for you. Shep and I have been talking, and we want to know what you'd like for our first child to call you. Because that will set the tone for what our other children call you."

"You mean I can't be Grandda to them too?" She asked him how that would work. "I don't know. I just thought with everyone calling me Grandda, it would be all right for the little ones to do the same."

"That settles that then. Grandda it is." He smiled at her, and asked what was really wrong. "I want this job. I want it so badly that I can almost taste it. I can do it. I know I can, but I don't want to go back on my word with Shep. I told him that I'd be here for him."

"Honey, I don't know if you know this or not, but everyone around you knows you want it. You complain so much about not having it that it makes us know that." She pouted at him. "You do that well, you know. But it doesn't change the fact that you're going to be in charge, and we're all as proud as can be about it. As for Shep. Harris, he'd only want you to be happy. That boy is so besotted with you that I think he'd do about anything for you to make you happy. He told me the other day that he wished you'd just take it. He knows you want it too."

"You think that's right? That he wants me to take it too?" Grandda said he'd never seen her so indecisive before. "Because this is important to a great many people. Not that I don't care what they want of me, but it's Shep and you that I want to do the right thing for most of all."

"Harris, you do it for yourself before you do something for anyone else. How else you going to be happy all the time if you're not doing what you want to do? You can't. You take that job and you keep this here country safe. They need you more than we do. You know why?" She shook her head at him. "Because we know that whatever you decide to do, you're going to be coming home to us every night that you can — we understand that. That is one of the reasons that you have to take it. So you can do right by us too."

"I'm going to do it." She felt the weight of the decision roll right off her. "Thank you, Grandda. You're the best sounding board that I've ever used."

It took her another hour to go over the barn. It didn't look like it had when she'd been growing up here. Her father had had horses — only two of them, but he'd loved them dearly. Harris wondered what had happened to them. When Shep joined her a little while later, she didn't go to him, but stood by where the stall had been — and was now being turned into a bathroom — and talked to him.

"The last Christmas that we had together as a family, my dad went all out. He'd never done that before. I'm not saying that we didn't have good Christmases. We always did, but we had a huge dinner and invited the local homeless shelter in to have a good meal with us." Shep told her that was a wonderful idea. "Yes. I don't know what made me think of it. Probably because I made a decision about the job. With your grandda."

"He told me. He said that he'd not had to talk you into taking it very hard. I think that he loves you more than me." She said that wasn't possible. "I think it is. He loves you as much as I do, and that's a great deal. Why are you out here? I thought the workers were done for the day."

"They are. I just wanted to come out and see what sort of progress they're making." She turned and looked at him. "What would I have done without you, Shep? I know that I'd be unhappy about what I was doing. More than likely dead, now that I think on it."

"Nah, you're a survivor. You can do anything and everything that you set your mind to. Are you ready to shift and have some fun?" She told him that she had a guest coming. "Oh? Anyone I know? I think by you calling them a guest that they're not someone that you know well. Am I right?"

"His name is Jason. I don't know if he has a last name or not, but he's a vampire. I've also decided to do what you suggested, and see if he can tell me if I am a vampire or something else. If I am and it's someone he knows, then he can tell me about them. Like if they're alive or not." He moved into the barn with her and held her in his arms. "He's here, I think. I can see him in the darkness."

"Hello, Harrison. It's been a very long time since I've seen

192

you." She nodded and introduced Jason to Shep. "I knew your mother well. She was a good friend of mine, and would allow me to sleep in her basement if I needed a quick and safe place to sleep. I was very sorry to hear of her passing."

"My brother is living there now. If you asked him, I'm sure that he'd gladly let you rest there if you wish." Jason said that he'd keep that in mind. "You're going to tell us what sort of magic that Harris holds? I have to admit, I hope that it's vampire. I know a little about your kind, but nothing about faeries."

"They are difficult to know, I'm afraid." He bowed before them before taking her hand. "It will not hurt you at all, my dear, but we will be connected. Are you all right with that? Is your spouse too?"

"I am all right with that. I know what it means for us to be connected. So if you'd not mind, I'd like a little of your blood as well. Just so we can be connected in the event that you need me." Jason agreed, and Shep did as well. "What do you need from me other than blood?"

"Nothing, my dear." He leaned over her hand, and she felt the small nip to her skin. When he was finished, he offered her his. Cutting open the vein on his wrist, Shep took a small sip, and then she did as well. When she staggered back, Jason laughed. "A bit of power is yours now. Let me tell you what I know."

# Chapter 14

James wasn't sure that he wanted to talk to his sons. So far as he was concerned, they'd been mean to their father, and he didn't think that was right. He was a changed man now, and they should be able to forgive him for being the way he was. James laughed a little, and thought that with Jill Ann gone, he had to be good. And the boys were bigger than him too. But they should be the forgiving kind to their daddy.

When he was allowed into the house, he could only marvel at it. His boy had done well for himself, and he should be able to fork over a little cash for his daddy. The smells that were coming from the other rooms were making his mouth water. James knew that there was beef involved in the meal, and that was all he thought about until Shep came down the stairs after the butler took his hat.

"Dad. I'm glad that you made it. I was just working on one of the bedrooms when they told me you were here. The others are in the living room. Just through here." He asked about his wife. "She'll be along. Dad, she's promised to not kill you if you behave yourself. You will, won't you? I don't want you to fuck this up."

"What a way to speak to me. I'm your father, and you'd best not forget it, Shep. I swear, kids nowadays, they sure don't have any respect for their elders." His own daddy came into the hall and asked him what sort of respect he had for him. "You can only get what you hand out, Daddy. Weren't you the one that said that to me all the time?"

"I did. And it didn't seem to stick to you very well. But we're not going to be nasty to each other, do you hear me, son? If you are, then you'd best be getting on out of here now."

James hated his father. He was a mean, grumpy old man, and he just hated the way that he treated him. Walking past his son and father, he entered the living room.

"Good Christ, this is huge. Can you imagine the parties that we can hold in here?" He'd forgotten that he wasn't going to bring up him living there with them, but now that he'd broken the ice, so to speak, he was going to do it now. "I could live here with you, son. You'd never know I was around. Well, except for mealtimes. You eat them all together?"

"Unless you know of a house someplace that is not on this property, there is no way in hell you're living around here. Hello, Grandda." Harris kissed his dad on the cheek and hugged the others. "I do hope you know that we're serious about this, James. We've all talked it over before you got here, and we've all decided that you've made your bed and you can lie in it or not. We're not going to house you."

"You are the worst kind of person that I've ever met." Harris thanked him. "It wasn't any compliment, damn it. I was telling you that I don't like you. You're rude, and too outspoken for this family."

"She's perfect." James rolled his eyes at his father. "She is. Just like Jill Ann was before you put her in an early grave. Had you been around she'd have not had to go out to the grocery in the middle of the night. It should have been you driving when that car came out of nowhere and hit her. You did that to this family."

He told his dad to shut up, he didn't know what the fuck he was talking about. His sons, all of them, stood up, and looked like they were ready to do battle. He told them that he didn't need their help. Rodney laughed.

"It wasn't you that we were going to protect, Father dear." There was a tone there that he didn't like, and said as much. "I don't care what you think of my tone. I'm a grown man with my own life. One you've had very little to do with. Not that I want you around now, because I was thrilled to death when Mom finally kicked your ass to the curb."

"She was hateful to me. All the time hiding money away so that I'd not be able to take it. I have to tell you, I surely thought that she'd be nicer to me when I hit her around. She was never like other women that were beaten into submission. She never learned her lesson." James laughed. "Well, she learned her lesson, didn't she?"

"What do you mean, son? What do you mean, she learned her lesson?" James knew that he'd said too much when they all stared at him. His father asked him again what he meant. "James, did you have something to do with your wife's death?"

"I did not." He hadn't, not really. He'd paid someone to do it. James looked around the room, and knew that the woman there knew something. "You think you're so high and mighty, don't you, missy? Well, you don't know shit. I don't think I want to live here anymore either."

"Tell them how you paid a man with the insurance money that you didn't have to kill Mom, Dad." James started to back away. "You knew that there wasn't any insurance money coming to you, didn't you? But that didn't stop you from having this man, Arthur Berry, to T-bone her out in the middle of nowhere so that she'd surely die before anyone would know. Then you killed him, because he was going to the police about what you made him do."

"You don't know what you're talking about. Get away from me, Shep. Before I call the police." James was in deep shit here. He was going to have to get out of here without any funds, because he had a feeling that asking them now was going to get him into more shit. "I'm leaving here. You all ruined it for me. I was going to have a pleasant dinner with my family, and now you've messed it up for you all."

"You're not going anywhere until you tell us why you murdered our mother." So they all knew, did they? First Shep, then Dean. There wasn't any way that he was going to live here with them either. "We found his body."

"What?" Dean repeated himself. "No, you're lying. There isn't any way that you did any such thing. You want to know why? You can't sniff out lye where I took him. I suppose next you're going to tell me that you found the car too. No way on that either. It's been parted out a long time ago."

"I work for the FBI. Did you know that, James?" He paled when she said that. "We have ways about us that make all kinds of thing come to light. Like the fact that the people that you donated the car to, they knew that it had been involved in a homicide, but since what they were doing wasn't legal, they left a note in the car about who had sold it to them and who they thought was involved in the murder of Jill Ann. We found it just this morning. The body was easy to find after that, too. You buried it right here on this land."

"There wasn't anyone living here. How the fuck did you find it? It had to be nothing but bones by now. Damn it, woman, if I had a gun right now, I'd blow your fucking head right off those shoulders of yours." She handed him a picture, and he sat down on the floor when he looked at it. "No. This isn't right. It's not fair at all."

The police entered the room then and put cuffs on him. James kept looking at the picture that had Arthur's name on it. The place he worked was there too. It was a little rotted, but he could make it out. He was read his rights and then dragged to the car. He didn't even get to have anyone handing him over some money.

They were all out on the porch when he was sitting in the back of the car. The cops were talking to them all like they were best friends. Well, he'd show them all—he wasn't saying another word. Besides, it was his word against theirs, and he was related to very rich people.

He was charged with two murders. Then they started adding on things like mutilation of a corpse. Insurance fraud, which he didn't understand. Threatening a federal officer, to which he pointed out that she was his daughter-in-law and that didn't count. They didn't listen, but just kept naming off things that he didn't have any idea where they got all their information from.

James was settled in a cell, but told not to get too comfortable. Like that was even possible with him having no beef dinner or a nice bed to lay down on. He was told that he was being transferred to a federal prison, because of the threat.

Then they told him that if he mentioned being her father-in-law again, they were going to put tape over his mouth.

At nearly dark, James heard someone coming down the hall. He didn't get up. If they were bringing him another meal, a good one this time, they'd have to ask him to take it. He wasn't about to be treated like he was some kind of bad guy.

It was Harris, dressed up in a nice suit. High heels just tall enough to make her legs all sexy looking. He wasn't ready to forgive her yet, but if she'd come to bail him out, he might be a little nicer to her. When she told him to stand up, he did so without hesitation. Her cat was stronger than his, he realized.

"You're a pain in the ass, did you know that?" He told her he was no such thing. "I'll be the judge of that. You're going to prison, James. For a very long time. And even if you live to be one hundred and fifty years old, you won't have shit to fall back on. I've made sure of that."

"What did you do to me?" Harris told him that it was no less than he deserved. "You're not the least bit nice, are you? What if I told Shep that you made a pass at me? You think he'd be so quick to take you back?"

"Me, make a pass at you?" She laughed long and hard, and he wanted to hit her for it. "I'd rather sleep with a crocodile than you. I'm sure that I'd be safer. But what I've done for you is this. You'll spend most of your days in solitude. I doubt very much that anyone would want to be around you for very long anyway. You'll get your three meals a day, and they'll be only what is required by law. A meat, vegetable, and a fruit. Drinks too, but only water."

"The meat will have to be steak. I don't want to ever have to eat bologna again. Nor do I want you to have them give me vegetables. You can substitute that out for some other kind of meat. I don't like water either." She told him too bad. "You'll do this for me. I'm related to you."

"Not anymore you're not. Once you go to where I'm having you sent, you'll be only a number to anyone. They'll call you that so often that you'll swear that it's your name. I've spoken to a federal judge, and we all agree that since you confessed to everything we have on you, there is no point in wasting the taxpayers' money on a trial. I'm sending you away for life without any chance of parole. You'll die behind bars." He stood up and shook the bars. "You're lucky that it's me that is giving you the sentence. Your sons wanted you to be strapped to an electric chair today. They told me that as far as they're concerned, you're already dead."

"You can't do this to me. I've done nothing wrong." She didn't even say a word to him. "Listen, we got off on the wrong foot, you and me. Why don't we start over and you forget all that other stuff? I won't even try and live with you."

"That's good, James, because you were never going to. There is something that Shep told me to tell you as well. Your grandchildren will never know of you. No one will tell them what sort of person you were. To them and your sons, you are already rotting in a grave. They also decided that you can be buried in the graveyard around the prison. With your number carved into the stone at your head, just like it is on the chest of your uniform." James staggered back from the bars, his heart hurting with the things she was saying to him. "Also, the name that you passed onto your son, Sheppard James Cartwright, will end with him. Shep is going to not name his sons after a monster such as you."

Harris must have left him at some point while he was thinking about what she'd said to him. The part about grandchildren, that hurt him the most. No little boys coming to sit on his lap? No one to call him Grandda? He'd never in all his years thought about them until just then. And now they were taken from him with a swipe of a hand, so to speak.

The lights went off. James had never been one to wear a watch, and he couldn't afford a cell phone, so he didn't have any idea what time it was. Lying on the cot, he thought about all the things that they'd accused him of, and decided that at some point someone was going to ask about him. He had friends that would care about him, even if his sons didn't.

But as the sun came up over the window in his cell, he hadn't thought of a single person that would be called a friend. There were people that he knew, but of late they had been avoiding him. Crossing the road to get away from him.

When the men came to get him that morning, he didn't even speak to them. James had been dealt a shitty hand, and it was all because of that Harris woman. The van ride was long, but it didn't bother him. He wished that he had someone to tell that he'd be gone for a while, but again, didn't know who that would be.

"Can I make a phone call?" He was denied that as well. "I just want to call my dad. Tell him where I am and that he needs to try and bail me out."

"There isn't any bail set for you, so it would do you little good. Also, I'm to remind you that your number from now on is seven-three-six-nine. You will be called that from now on. You don't answer, then things will not go well for you. Understand?"

He was in his cell before he realized those numbers meant something to him. Well, not meant anything, he thought, but he knew them. They were Jill Ann's birthday. July third sixty-nine.

For the first time in all his life, James cried. Not for the loss of his wife and children, but because no one had loved him. Not ever. When he got out of here, and he would, he was going to make them love him. He'd tell them that everyday that it was their duty to love him. He was their dad. Yes sir, that was what he was going to do when he got out of here. He was fucking going to be loved.

### Before You Go...

# HELP AN AUTHOR

## *write a review*

# THANK YOU!

Share your voice and help guide other readers to these wonderful books. Even if it's only a line or two your reviews help readers discover the author's books so they can continue creating stories that you'll love. Login to your favorite retailer and leave a review. Thank you.

AWARD WINNING, BESTSELLING AUTHOR

Kathi Barton, winner of the Pinnacle Book Achievement award as well as a best-selling author on Amazon and All Romance books, lives in Nashport, Ohio with her husband Paul. When not creating new worlds and romance, Kathi and her husband enjoy camping and going to auctions. She can also be seen at county fairs with her husband who is an artist and potter.

Her muse, a cross between Jimmy Stewart and Hugh Jackman, brings her stories to life for her readers in a way that has them coming back time and again for more. Her favorite genre is paranormal romance with a great deal of spice. You can visit Kathi online and drop her an email if you'd like. She loves hearing from her fans. aaronskiss@gmail.com.

Follow Kathi on her blog: http://kathisbartonauthor. blogspot.com/

www.ingramcontent.com/pod-product-compliance
Lightning Source LLC
Chambersburg PA
CBHW020621180626
46810CB00007B/2887